## 'Now what's wrong?'

He pulled her to one side when she would have gone marching on.

'I can please myself what I do in my own time,' Fiona returned crisply.

Rory's frown cleared and he laughed. 'So that's what this is all about. Look, if anyone needs their hand slapped, then I slap it. Where the well-being of patients is concerned I let no one get away with sloppiness. Outside of work, though, we can be friends. All right?'

'No, not all right!'

**Dear Reader**

We have a good variety for you this month! Alice Grey gives us an insight into health visiting and the problems people can encounter. In MAJOR INCIDENT, Grace Read explores the hectic world of Casualty where Rory thinks he's too old for Fiona! We introduce new author Carol Wood, who brings veterinarian work back to the medical list—we think she's good and hope you do too. And Judith Worthy takes us to coastal Australia, where Lee and Trent have a lot to sort out after twelve years apart. Enjoy!

*The Editor*

**Grace Read** has had a lifelong love-affair with nursing. Starting as a Red Cross nurse in a London hospital during the war, she went on to do her general training in the Midlands. Marriage and a baby ended that career, but she retains a keen interest in the profession. Her youngest daughter is a nursing sister and keeps Grace abreast of modern trends, vetting her novels for medical accuracy.

# MAJOR INCIDENT

BY

## GRACE READ

## MILLS & BOON LIMITED
ETON HOUSE    18–24 PARADISE ROAD
RICHMOND    SURREY    TW9 1SR

For Sister Margaret Johnson RGN
with love and gratitude.

*First published in Great Britain 1993
by Mills & Boon Limited*

© Grace Read 1993

*Australian copyright 1993
Philippine copyright 1993
This edition 1993*

ISBN 0 263 78067 8

*Set in 10 on 12 pt Linotron Baskerville
03-9303-54384*

*Typeset in Great Britain by Centracet, Cambridge
Made and printed in Great Britain*

# CHAPTER ONE

IT HAD been a gusty sort of morning, the kind that rattled the windows of the large Victorian mansion which had been converted into flatlets for qualified staff of the Thames Valley Memorial Hospital. The first drops of rain spattered the glass as Fiona gazed out absently while finishing her lunchtime coffee before reporting for duty.

Her thoughts were with Craig. His letter had been awaiting her when she arrived back after spending a week with her mother in Brussels. Craig wrote that his contract at the Florida hospital was nearly up and he hoped to be back in England in six weeks' time. *Then*, he went on significantly, there were important things they would have to discuss.

Actually Fiona had found it something of a relief when, almost a year ago, Craig had decided to try his luck in the USA after failing to get promotion to Charge Nurse at the West London hospital where they had both trained. It had been a convenient way of damping down their affair without hostility. Promising to write regularly was an easy option, and she had hoped he might find someone else in the meantime, or at least cool off towards her. Now she didn't know what to think.

Shrugging her slim shoulders, she decided there was little point in worrying about it until the time came. Meanwhile duty called, and, slipping her fawn leather jacket over her white uniform dress, she gathered up shoulder-bag, umbrella and car keys.

It was barely a ten-minute drive to the Memorial Hospital, but by the time Fiona arrived the fitful drizzle had become a deluge. For a few moments she stayed in her car, hoping the storm would ease off, but with time creeping on she had eventually to make a dash for it. Umbrella aloft, she was sprinting the two hundred yards from the car park to Casualty when a sudden, furious gust of wind tore the umbrella from her hands. It whirled through the air and bounced off the bonnet of the red BMW about to park in one of the places reserved for the medical staff.

Dashing for the shelter of the canopy over the entrance, Fiona pulled a mournful face as she pushed back her bedraggled fair hair and regarded the fate of her property. True, the driver jumped on his brakes and backed a little before getting out to see what damage he had done.

He hurried to join her under cover. 'That's had it, I regret to say,' he remarked.

There was the slightest trace of a Scottish burr in the rich, deep voice, and Fiona's eyes flitted from the mangled remains on the forecourt to the dark-haired man looking down at her from his impressive height.

She swallowed, her eyes wide. It had to be him, didn't it? Of course he had changed somewhat in eleven years. He was leaner, and bronzed, and the thick dark hair had receded a little at the temples. But those devastatingly dark blue eyes were unforgettable. She had a kind of storybook memory of Rory Kinross which was a pleasure to recall. She had been thirteen then, and he at university and full of natural charm. But it was quite evident that he hadn't recognised her, so all she could do now was to take a deep breath and find some kind of voice.

'Yes,' she agreed with a tentative smile. 'Not your fault. . .just one of those things.'

'Bit of an optimist, weren't you, putting it up in this gale?'

'It was either that or get drowned. We don't all have privileged parking spots.' Oh, dear! The moment she'd said that she wished she hadn't, and she didn't know why she had, unless it was the patronising twist to his otherwise agreeable mouth. That, and being completely thrown by the sudden bounding of her pulse.

Rory Kinross simply drew in his firm chin and looked down at her from under his straight dark brows, a glint of amusement lighting his keen blue eyes.

'Sorry. . . I didn't mean that to sound the way it did,' she put in hastily.

'Let's blame the weather.' He flashed her a forgiving smile. 'Are you coming in this way?' She nodded, and he ushered her ahead of him, then strode off briskly in the direction of the sister's office.

At a slower pace Fiona made for the staff-room to deposit her things. Her heart was still drumming disturbingly as her mind sped back those eleven years. It was her brother James, then at London University, who had brought his handsome friend home for part of the summer vacation. And although he had been a tease, the fact that Rory Kinross had not been above taking notice of a shy adolescent had won her young heart.

That was the one and only time they had met. The intervening years had sent them all in different directions. When Fiona was sixteen their father had died, and later, when their mother had remarried and moved to Brussels, James's house in Hampstead had become Fiona's home base. Consequently she had heard occasional news of Rory, although he had returned to his native Edinburgh. She remembered there had been a tragedy in his life—a girlfriend of his dying after a climbing accident.

'Fiona! Oh, I'm glad I'm on with you.' Bea White, a married staff nurse recently returned part-time after maternity leave, exclaimed with pleasure on seeing her. 'There are so many new people since I was last here. Ghastly day, isn't it?'

'Vile. Still, perhaps it'll keep the customers away,' Fiona returned cheerfully. Taking off her leather jacket, she gave it a quick shake before hanging it in her locker. 'I just met a guy I think I knew in my dim and distant past,' she said, reaching for a paper towel to dry her moist face and her damp hair. 'Rory Kinross. . .does that name ring any bells with you?'

Bea paused in the act of positioning her blue-bordered cap on her brown mid-length bob. 'Kinross? Yes, he's the new Cas consultant. Orthopaedic whizz-kid just back from foreign parts. What do you mean, you think you knew him?'

'Goes way back to my schooldays,' Fiona explained. 'My brother's ten years older than me, and they were buddies at university. Rory spent a weekend with us once and. . .once seen, never forgotten.'

The other girl laughed. 'Know what you mean! Did he remember you?'

'Well, he wouldn't, would he? I had no bosom to speak of then, and braces on my teeth. No, he would have walked right past me if he hadn't managed to run over my umbrella just now.' Fiona pulled a comb through her honey-blonde locks and tucked curling stray tendrils behind her ears before fastening her own cap into place with white hair-grips.

'You going to remind him?'

Fiona looked uncertain. 'I'll see how it goes.' She pinned on her name-badge. 'Well, let's see what this mournful Sunday has got in store for us.'

With the late shift assembled in Sister Bland's office, the early shift nurses went to lunch. There followed a quick résumé of patients in the department at the time before the sister assigned the staff to their various duties.

'I'll leave the bleep with you, Fiona,' she said. 'Dr Hadlow is with Mr Kinross at the moment, discussing Miss Morley's X-rays. She's the eighty-year-old lady with the Colles' fracture, and he'd like her admitted for a few days. She's got badly bruised knees as well.' Sister Bland gave a sigh. 'The poor old soul lives with another old lady who's got Parkinson's, and it appears they don't have any help whatsoever. I've called their GP and he's promised to look into it. Check that Miss Morley's OK, will you, Fiona? She's in cubicle four.'

Sister Bland bustled off to her own lunch and Fiona went to seek out the patient in question. She found an anxious-looking, extremely thin, sparse-haired woman in an examination gown, propped up on the bed nursing her injured arm in its sling.

'Hello, Miss Morley,' Fiona greeted her in a friendly way. 'Are you all right for the moment. . .anything I can do for you?'

The patient gave a wan smile. 'I'd love a cup of tea, dear, but I suppose that's not allowed for the time being.'

'I'm afraid not.' Fiona eyed her sympathetically. 'The doctors are studying your X-rays at present. You'll probably be going to Theatre soon to have your wrist sorted out.'

'I am rather worried about the lady I live with,' Miss

Morley confided. 'She relies on me absolutely, you see. She's quite helpless. I only went out to post a letter, and this happened. I tripped up a kerb and people telephoned for an ambulance. She'll be wondering where on earth I am.'

'Well, Sister did tell me she'd been in touch with your GP about that,' Fiona began, when the curtains parted to admit the casualty officer accompanied by Rory Kinross.

Dr Adrian Hadlow, a well-liked and diligent young medic, pushed his spectacles further up on his nose and threw Fiona a toothy grin before addressing the patient. 'Miss Morley, this is Mr Kinross, our orthopaedic consultant, who's been studying your X-rays.'

The consultant smiled at the old lady while checking the radial pulse in her uninjured wrist. 'We think it best for you to stay in for a few days after your wrist has been put in plaster,' he told her.

'Oh, dear! Is that really necessary?' she queried.

'I should prefer it. You'll need a general anaesthetic, and we'll want to make sure you can cope when you go home. Is there a problem?'

Miss Morley's bottom lip quivered. 'We-ell, as I was saying to Nurse. . . I don't know how my friend will manage.'

His dark brows raised in question, Rory Kinross glanced towards Fiona, who volunteered, 'The lady she lives with has Parkinson's, but I understand Sister's been in touch with their doctor about it.'

The consultant's steady gaze lingered on Fiona for a moment and she felt her cheeks warm under his scrutiny. 'Confirm that, will you?' he murmured. His eyes travelled to her name badge. 'We shall hold Nurse Rogers personally responsible for your peace of mind, Miss

Morley.' Turning to Dr Hadlow, he added, 'I'll arrange for the bed in Paget Ward. She can have her pre-med now and I'll do the reduction in one of the emergency theatres.' With a kindly glance towards the patient, he left them.

Writing up the required premedication, the casualty officer chatted with Fiona. 'I expect this all seems very tame stuff to Kinross after his experiences in the Third World.'

'Where's he been, then?' Fiona tried to sound only casually interested, although her head was teeming with questions.

'Bangladesh, with a Red Cross set-up out there. I must say I admire people who do that kind of thing, but I've got no sense of adventure.' Adrian stretched in his chair and laid down his ballpoint. 'Too fond of my mod cons.'

'I'm not the pioneering kind, either,' Fiona said, laughing. 'Anyway, it's a good thing we don't all want to go dashing off to wherever. Some of us have to man the home front.' She paused. 'When did he start here? Kinross, I mean.'

'About ten days ago. He took over when McPhail left. I believe they'd worked together in Edinburgh before Kinross went abroad.'

'I wonder why Rory didn't go back to Edinburgh?' Fiona murmured, half to herself.

'No job there, perhaps, if he wanted promotion,' Adrian suggested. 'And how long have you been on Christian-name terms with him?' he added with a dry grin.

'Oh, I'm not really—long story. Tell you about it some time. Right now I'd better give this pre-med and get Miss Morley ready for Theatre.'

\* \* \*

At the first opportunity when Sister Bland came back from lunch Fiona decided it might be as well to report the consultant's remarks about the matter of Miss Morley's dependent companion.

'Well, I told their GP—spoke to him myself—so it's up to him now,' Molly Bland said. 'We've got our own work to do.' And with that Fiona had to be satisfied.

The afternoon passed busily with a steady flow of problems, none of which required the expertise of Rory Kinross, so that thoughts of the charismatic Scot were pushed to the back of her mind. She dealt with a sprained ankle, a distraught mother whose toddler had fallen from an upstairs window and miraculously suffered only a graze, a man with a severe nose-bleed and a young woman with a badly cut hand.

Fiona was adept at suturing, and Rosemary, a third-year student, was glad of the chance to see how the laceration should be handled.

'I'll give you a couple of injections to numb the area before we start, Mrs Parry,' Fiona reassured the anxious patient. 'This is the worst part,' she consoled, skilfully injecting lignocaine on either side of the gaping wound. 'There, that's all. We'll wait a few moments and then the stitching itself won't hurt a bit.'

The girl, who had been biting her lips, sniffed back a tear and gave a tremulous laugh. 'Call me Roma—I can't get used to being Mrs Parry. We're only just back from our honeymoon. There I was slicing our first Sunday roast when the wretched knife slipped.'

'You'd better get him to do it next time, then,' Rosemary said, laughing.

Fiona attempted the first suture. 'You're not feeling this? Fine. Where did you go for your honeymoon?' she asked, carrying on with her task.

To the accompaniment of light-hearted small talk the rest of the repair was soon done, a protective covering applied, and Roma Parry went on her way, comforted by her solicitous new husband.

Sighing, Rosemary gazed after them. 'I went to a silver-wedding party last night. I wonder if that pair will last twenty-five years?'

Fiona gave a non-committal shrug and cleaned up her trolley. She had a disturbing feeling that Craig might be going to ask her to make the final commitment when they met again. And she certainly didn't want to do that. Not yet. Not ever—to Craig. A fun affair was one thing. Marriage was quite another.

At four-thirty Sister Bland went off duty, leaving Fiona in charge. The crash call came around six-thirty as it was beginning to grow dark. A twenty-year-old youth had gone over the handles of his motorbike, the ambulance station reported. They suspected a dislocated hip and would be delivering him in about fifteen minutes.

Fiona passed the message to Adrian, who groaned. 'If there's anything I loathe it's dislocations. That means getting hold of Kinross again. . .and he said he had an evening appointment. . .'

'Tough!' Fiona said without too much sympathy.

The casualty officer threw her a sideways glance. 'Do I detect a lack of fellow feeling?'

She grinned. 'Not really, but I don't know how he's going to react, do I, after having his plans messed up? Remember McPhail? He used to take it out on everyone.' Not that she thought Rory Kinross could possibly be as irascible as his predecessor had sometimes been, but she had yet to discover what kind of man he had become now that he was at the top of his profession. And it was difficult to know how, and when, or even if she should remind him of their past connection.

'I'll leave you to chase him up, then. Bea and I will meet the ambulance,' she finished.

Grabbing a trolley, the nurses went to the double doors to await the arrival of their patient.

'The rain's stopped, thank goodness,' Bea said, gazing out at the glistening wet, leaf-strewn forecourt.

In a few moments the ambulance swished to a halt, the doors were opened up and one of the paramedics came to give Fiona the essential details. 'The lad's name's Mike Hills. We've had to leave him on his side, in the same position as we found him. There was too much pain to move him. . .he's quite shocked, so we've put him on a Haemaccel drip. OK?'

She nodded in acknowledgement. 'Fine, thanks.'

The casualty, a large youth, was eased gently on to the trolley, still lying in his awkward side posture. His face was pale and sweaty and contorted with pain. He wore heavy, expensive-looking leathers, and the nurses exchanged glances, knowing that the costly gear was going to have to be cut off before anything could be done to help him.

'Hello, Mike,' Fiona said gently, taking his hand as they wheeled him along to an examination cubicle. 'How did this happen?'

'Tree branch. . .blew down in front of me,' the lad got out between sighing breaths. 'No way. . . I could avoid . . .crashing into it.'

'No other vehicle involved?' Adrian prompted, joining them. He checked the boy's pulse and made a few preliminary observations. 'Seems to me you've got a dislocation there, old son. We'll have to confirm that by

X-ray, of course. But all this lovely gear's going to have to come off first.'

Fiona reached for the workmanlike scissors kept especially for such problems and began cutting up the seam of the tight leathers. 'Terribly sorry about this, but there's no other way we can do it, to save you further pain or injury,' she explained.

'Do what you like. . . I'm past caring,' Mike returned weakly. He winced with pain at the unavoidable movement caused by their efforts. 'Can't stand much more of this. You sure it's not broken?'

'Very painful things, dislocations. It's the contraction of the muscles that does it,' Adrian explained.

'We'll get an ice-pack on it as soon as we get you out of your trousers,' Fiona promised.

She handed the scissors to Bea to do her share of the cutting, and when at last the leggings were able to be carefully removed an immensely swollen and deformed hip joint was revealed.

'Seems conclusive,' the casualty officer murmured. 'Right, Fiona, on with your ice-pack while I make the necessary checks, then we'll give him some pethidine to tide him over until Kinross arrives.'

The essentials gone through as speedily as possible, Mike was wheeled along to X-ray and the injury confirmed.

'No fracture,' Fiona told him reassuringly. 'At least once this is put back into place you shouldn't be out of action for too long.'

'How long is that?' he wanted to know, more relaxed since the pain-killing drug had taken some effect.

'Maybe a week, all being well.' She wheeled him into the emergency theatre, leaving him in Bea's comforting care while she went to deliver the X-ray plates to Adrian.

The nurses had been talking to the boy about whom they should contact, since he had no next of kin and lived in a bed-sit. He had been on his way to meet his girlfriend, and Fiona had promised to advise her of the accident. Concentrating on the patient, thoughts of Rory Kinross were furthest from her mind. Then, as she entered the doctor's office, there he was, perched on a corner of the desk and elegant in evening dress. His powerful presence caught her unprepared, startling her into silence.

Rising, he reached out for the package in her hands. 'Are these what we're waiting for? Thank you.' He slid the films from their large brown envelope and placed them into the viewing screen.

Fiona watched and waited while the doctors talked. She was quite convinced that Rory hadn't even noticed her as a person. To him she was just an impersonal pair of hands bringing the information he required. Which was just as it should be really, and she had no cause to feel peeved. He had been perfectly polite. Nevertheless she sighed, studying the back of his shapely dark head as he expounded on the procedure to be followed.

'The reduction may be difficult. Ideally it should be done under a general anaesthetic, but you say he ate recently?' The consultant's dark brows rose in question.

Adrian looked to Fiona for confirmation and she nodded. 'About an hour ago, he said.'

'So we'll have to give him Entonox plus-plus and some more pethidine IV.' He suddenly directed a searching glance towards Fiona. 'And do you know why we shouldn't risk holding up the reduction, Nurse?'

The unexpected question caught her off guard. She had been miles away, thinking how impressive he was and wondering who would be missing out on his company that night. She swallowed, momentarily lost for words. Of course she knew why—she was an experienced casualty nurse, for goodness' sake. But the textbook definition of the orthopaedic emergency just would not come. 'Oh—er. . .' she began, after taking a deep breath.

'It's because we can't risk avascular necrosis to the head of the femur. . .where the red blood cells are produced,' he prompted with a patient smile. 'Right, Adrian, let's get on with it. I'll go and have a word with the lad while you make preparations.'

The reduction was not an aseptic process since there was no external wound to complicate matters, but it required considerable strength and skill on the consultant's part to guide the femur head back into its socket. Although not able to be fully anaesthetised, with the aid of the gas and air machine and a relaxing injection the patient was kept comfortable during the proceedings. After a further X-ray to confirm correct positioning, the limb was immobilised with strapping and a happier young man transferred to the orthopaedic wing for a few days.

It was almost nine o'clock before Fiona had time to make that telephone call to Mike's girlfriend.

'He's comfortable now and sleeping off his sedation, so there's no point in you visiting tonight,' she advised. 'I'm sure he'd love to see you tomorrow, though. Ring the ward in the morning to find out how he is.'

The night staff had already arrived and one of them brought Fiona a welcome mug of coffee while she wrote up her report on the patients they had treated. 'Thanks, pal,' she said. 'Oh, have the doctors had some?'

'Yes, Bea saw to that,' she was told.

Fiona carried on with her writing, satisfied that

nothing had been left undone. Kinross deserved more than a coffee, she thought, for the excellent work he had put in that night. She chewed the end of her ballpoint reflectively for a moment, her thoughts back in the emergency theatre where, shirt-sleeves rolled up past his elbows, Rory had toiled to manipulate the femur head back to its rightful place, afterwards checking to make sure that the sciatic nerve had not been injured. Yes, he deserved his privileged parking spot, she mused, with a private smile.

Her handover report given, she was tidying away some forms before going off duty when the consultant himself walked by the office. He paused on seeing her there and, glancing up, she smiled in his direction.

'Can I help you?' She was less inhibited now that the problems of the night were behind them and knowing that she'd acquitted herself well despite not being able to drum up a prompt answer to his technical question.

'Not exactly.' He came further in so that they were not overheard by others of the staff. 'You're off now, are you?'

'Yes, in a minute.'

'And it isn't raining now, so you won't need an umbrella. But you must buy yourself another and let me have the bill.'

Ah, so she wasn't just a pair of hands—he had remembered her. 'Oh, forget it,' she returned brightly. 'It wasn't my one and only. And it could have gone under anyone's wheels.'

'But it happened to go under mine. . .and I prefer to make amends.' He smiled disarmingly, his teeth pearly-white against his tanned skin.

There was delightful chaos in the pit of her stomach as their eyes met and held. She was almost on the point of mentioning their past connections when his smile faded.

'And the next time I ask you to do something, kindly do it, will you?' he said.

Fiona's mouth gaped. What hadn't she done? 'Sorry? I don't understand——'

'I asked you to make sure Miss Morley's invalid friend was being looked after.'

'Well, I——' she begun, but he interrupted again.

'Fortunately something prompted me to make my own check, and I found that no one had been near the house. Oh, it's sorted out now. But I shouldn't have to do everything myself in this so-called civilised country. Goodnight.'

With that he strode away, not waiting for explanations, leaving Fiona on the point of exploding.

'He's got a nerve!' she exclaimed indignantly to Bea in the staff-room later, removing her cap and putting it in her locker. 'I *did* check that Molly had called Miss Morley's GP, and she said she had and it was out of our hands. What more could I do? Who the hell does he think he is, anyway?'

Bea was of a placid disposition and took the peccadilloes of the medical profession in her stride. She chuckled. 'Well, sorry you've had to take the can back, but I'm glad we've got someone prepared to move his shoulders to get things done around here. Molly's a dear soul, but she's not exactly dynamic, is she?'

Fiona grunted as she kicked off her white duty shoes and pulled on her fashion boots. 'I expect I got the fall-out because he had to cancel his date. Men! You won't think it so funny if you ever get on the wrong side of him.'

Smiling at Fiona's aggrieved expression, Bea declared,

'Being a mum now, I've got far more important things to worry about than crusty consultants.'

'Yes, that puts it in perspective.' Fiona's natural good humour returned and she also laughed. 'I shall phone my brother tonight and tell him what I think of his old buddy. You know, as I remember him he was terrific fun. Of course, it was a long time ago, and life does things to people,' she reflected. 'I wonder if James knew about Rory coming to work here? If so, he might have warned me.'

# CHAPTER TWO

THE first thing Fiona did on arriving home that evening was to ring her brother's number to find out if he had known that Rory was to be working at the Memorial Hospital. She was doomed to disappointment when her only contact was with an answering machine. There was the usual polite invitation to leave her number and her call would be returned as soon as possible.

'Oh, blow you, James,' she began, feeling thoroughly frustrated. 'This is your ever-loving sister. Why aren't you there when I want you? I'm back from Brussels. Call me soon, I want to talk. Love to Debs.'

That off her chest, she popped across the corridor to see if her neighbour, Lois, was in. There were six senior nurses with self-contained flatlets in this one-time imposing family residence, and, living opposite each other, Lois and Fiona had become firm friends. It also happened that Lois was a staff nurse on Orthopaedics and very likely to have had dealings with Rory Kinross, which might prove informative.

Suddenly Fiona was eager to find out all she could about her brother's old college chum. What, for instance, had prompted him to go to the Third World? Was it an altruistic desire to help the less fortunate, or was it an attempt to come to terms with that tragedy in his own life? People were motivated in all kinds of ways. Take Craig, for example. It was feeling piqued at being passed over for promotion which had made him look overseas.

But Rory Kinross gave the impression of great strength of character; hardly the type to act out of pique.

Fiona's knock brought Lois to the door, long brown hair in tumbled disarray over the shoulders of her pink bathrobe. 'Hi!' she exclaimed in pleased surprise. 'Come on in. When did you get back?'

'Late last night, actually. I've done a day's work since then.' Fiona sank into an easy-chair while Lois scooped a pile of magazines off another and folded her long legs into it.

'Had a good time?'

'Mmm. Not madly exciting, but nice to see my mum. And she fed me too well.'

Lois grinned. 'You should worry. What else did you do besides eat?'

'Went out a few times with my young stepbrother Miles. He's only just eighteen but really good company. We went to Waterloo—there's a church near there with memorials to the fallen.' Fiona's thoughts went back. 'And some of the soldiers were so young—just boys like Miles. It made me really sad.'

Lois twisted a strand of her hair. 'I know. . .and not much the average guy can do about it. . .except people like Kinross who go and pick up the pieces.'

'What do you think of him?' Fiona asked casually.

'An improvement on McPhail, that's for sure. Do you know what? He actually made a domiciliary visit to this old lady because one of his patients was worried about her!'

Fiona was wide-eyed. 'You mean. . . Miss Morley. . . the Colles' fracture?'

'Yep!' Lois nodded. 'He arranged for this friend she lives with to go into the Cottage Hospital for the time being. Not many of the top brass would personally put themselves out like that, would they?'

'So that's what he did,' murmured Fiona, half to herself. She jumped up from her chair. 'I'd better get back to my place, Lo—I'm expecting a phone call. Come on over and I'll tell you a story while I make us a bacon sandwich.'

Her friend laughed. 'Sounds intriguing. I'm all ears.'

Over their snack supper Fiona explained how Rory Kinross was a shadowy figure from the past. 'Which is why I'm waiting for this call from James,' she said. 'I mean, with Rory being A and E consultant here, how do I treat him? It's a bit delicate, isn't it? I can't say I really know him. . .although I do. And he's already bawled me out for not checking out Miss Morley's friend, but I could hardly go over Sister's head when she told me she'd done it.'

'You'll have to play it by ear,' Lois advised. 'I'll admit he likes his orders followed to the letter, but he's got all the staff of Paget dreamy-eyed.' She laughed. 'Well, you must admit he's gorgeous. It's that combination of mildness and steely authority which makes him so fascinating, I suppose.'

Munching her bacon sandwich, Fiona made no comment. Lois didn't know the half of it; the way just being in the consultant's presence made her nerve-endings tingle. And the less she told anyone about that, the better. After all, Rory was eleven years older than she was, and at the top of his profession. Subconsciously, it seemed, he had been the blueprint for Prince Charming since her childhood days. But that was all rather fanciful, wasn't it? High time she left that kind of romantic nonsense behind.

The two girls had parted company before the hoped-for telephone call came. And it wasn't her brother on the line; it was his live-in partner, Deborah. With Deborah also being in the nursing world, the two girls had much in common.

'James is away in California attending a dental conference,' Deborah told his sister. 'They certainly know how to choose their venues, don't they?' she laughed. 'He'll be home tomorrow, Fiona. Was it anything important?'

'Not really important, just interesting. There's a friend of his from way back who's just started work at the Memorial here—Rory Kinross. I wondered if James knew?'

'Oh, Rory. I don't know about that. There was a message from him on the answerphone too, but he wasn't in when I rang back.' Herself a sister at the local hospital, Deborah went on to say that she had just come home from a party for one of her staff who was getting married.

'So when are you and James going to tie the knot?' Fiona prompted. 'If you don't hurry up I'll be too old to be a bridesmaid, and I've never been one yet.'

Deborah laughed. 'Well, we both value our independence but, maybe, if we decide to start a family. . .'

'You'll make my mother ecstatic,' Fiona said.

Another day went by and Fiona had still not heard from her brother, or had personal contact again with Rory, although he looked in on the minor injuries clinic each morning for a short time. He was quite satisfied with re-dressings of old wounds to be done by the trained nurses.

On Wednesday morning Fiona treated a burned leg which she had dealt with regularly for the past two months. Now she was satisfied that the patient was fit for discharge. 'That looks fine now,' she told him. 'No need for you to come here any more. If it needs another dressing your doctor's practice nurse should be able to deal with it.'

'Righto, love,' the man said. 'That'll certainly be more convenient than making this journey every time. But thanks. I shall miss my visits here. It's been a real tonic just coming to see you.'

'That's made my day, although I don't believe a word of it,' Fiona told him, smiling. She cleaned up her trolley and went out to find her next patient.

The door to the consultant's office stood open as she would have passed by. Sitting at his desk in immaculate charcoal-grey suit, his dark head bent over some papers, he happened to glance up and see her. 'Nurse Rogers. . . will you spare me a moment, please. And shut the door behind you,' he added as she went in.

The discerning blue eyes swept over her. Oh, dear, she thought, her pulse bounding, now what haven't I done?

Rory Kinross leaned back in his chair, taking in the picture of a heart-shaped face framed in pale gold hair and the sprinkling of freckles across the bridge of a neat nose. 'Sit down.' He motioned her to the chair opposite. 'Why didn't you tell me who you were?' he asked, his deep voice mildly amused.

Her tension relaxed as it became clear that someone must have put him wise. Her own eyes sparkled impishly as she touched her identity badge. 'As it says. . . I'm Staff Nurse Rogers.'

His air of mock severity was belied by the smile which broke through. 'You know what I mean, young Eff. I *knew* there was a touch of *déjà vu* about those freckles, but I couldn't remember where we'd met before.'

She laughed softly, savouring the pleasure of the years rolling back. 'Oh, come on, you didn't have a clue it was me. And only James has ever called me Eff, so I suppose you've been talking to him?'

Rory nodded. 'He rang me last night. I do remember he mentioned some years ago that you were going into nursing, but I hardly expected to find you here.' His steady gaze was sending delightful shivers down her spine. 'Well, well!' he murmured at length. 'You've certainly changed since the last time we met. A leggy little menace you were then.'

'Thanks! At least I wasn't totally forgettable,' she returned jauntily.

'That's very true.'

They took stock of each other, both smiling. Then he sighed. 'Much as I'd like to continue this absorbing subject I haven't the time right now. But if I'm not to be allowed to buy you a new umbrella, may I take you out to dinner? Then you can fill me in on your progress to womanhood. Could you manage this evening?'

Decisively Fiona shook her head. 'Sorry.' She had no other plans, but it was best not to be too readily available, wasn't it? Besides, she wanted to talk to James first. 'I could make tomorrow.'

He consulted his desk diary for a moment, then nodded. 'Where shall I pick you up?'

'Sycamore Grange. . .do you know it? It's near to where Adrian Hadlow lives in the medics' quarters.'

'I'll find it. Shall we say eight o'clock?'

His telephone interrupting, she signalled her agreement and left.

'And what are you looking so pleased about?' Bea drawled, seeing her come from the consultant's office. 'Kinross now in favour, is he?'

'Getting to be,' Fiona said with a quiet smile. 'My brother put him in the picture last night. He's taking me out to dinner tomorrow.' She chuckled at Bea's arch expression. 'And you can take that look off your face. It's a kind of paternalistic gesture, I imagine. I wouldn't put it past my brother to ask Rory to keep a friendly eye on me.'

And she discovered that this was not far from the truth when she at last managed to speak to her brother later in the day.

'Well, who'd have thought my old mate would finally end up on your doorstep?' breezed James. 'I suppose you didn't see that piece on him in one of the medical journals recently, about the sterling work he was doing out East, especially among crippled children?'

'No, but I should like to, if you can find it for me. James. . .' Fiona paused. 'Tell me about that girlfriend of his who died. What exactly happened?'

'Oh, that. It started with a climbing accident in the Cairngorms. Corinne had a disastrous fall and was paralysed from the waist down. Rory stood by her, but she couldn't face life in a wheelchair, and a year later she ended it. . . OD'd on diazepam, I believe. It was catastrophic for him at the time.'

Fiona was surprised to find a lump in her throat. 'I— it must have been. How long ago was that?'

'Since she died? Must be two years, I think. I don't know exactly. They were living in Edinburgh then.'

'Do you think he joined that medical mission as a kind of. . .exorcism?'

'Who knows? I only hope I'm never faced with that kind of problem.' Her brother's voice took on a lighter note. 'My biggest headache to date is hoping my young sister knows how to take care of herself in this big bad world. Anyway, now I've got Rory on the spot to look out for you.'

'*James*! You didn't say anything like that to him, I hope?'

He chuckled. 'Not in so many words, but he knows I've always felt—well, *in loco parentis* for you since Mum went off to Brussels.'

'Oh, I could slaughter you!' Fiona exploded. 'When will you get it into your head that I'm not a two-year-old? I hold down a responsible job these days.'

'Yes, I know, kid. You're a clever girl. I'm proud of you,' he went on, teasing.

'OK, you can stop pontificating. I don't know how Debs puts up with you, you're getting so stuffy.'

'Not only does she put up with me. She's at last agreed to marry me.'

Fiona squealed with delight. 'She has? And about time. When?'

'No details yet. We'll let you know. I'll be asking Rory to be my best man. Now you treat him with due respect, Eff. He's a great guy.'

'Listen, I don't need advice from you on how to behave, chum.'

They concluded on a laughing note, but all Fiona could think about that night was the tragedy that had hit Rory Kinross. In their work they were accustomed to meeting tragedy—other people's—and the difficult task of trying to be supportive and comforting. But how did you cope when it hit home? Her only experience of the death of a loved one was when her father had died of lung cancer. They had known the end was coming, but even so it had been heart-rending when it happened.

Four years later her mother had remarried, something Fiona found hard to accept. Even though she was a second-year student nurse and living away from home at the time, she deplored the disintegration of the old family background.

'It's the best thing that could have happened, Eff,' James consoled her. 'It doesn't mean she loves Dad any the less, but you can't condemn her to a life of memories. You've virtually left the nest now, and I left years ago. Be glad she's found a decent guy to share her life with. And you can always come and stay with me on your days off.'

In the end it had worked out well. Fiona had grown to accept her stepfather, Paul, for the decent man he was, and his young son Miles had helped to fill the gap in her mother's life now that her own family was grown and independent.

None of which was in any way like the trauma Rory Kinross had faced. Now that she knew the details she would at least be aware of delicate ground and avoid stirring up painful memories when she went out to dinner with him.

Fiona was on an early the following day. It started quietly enough, the department being well staffed with the addition of two students and two extra staff nurses doing the Critical Care Course.

One of the students was assigned to Fiona to instruct in the cleaning and restocking of the theatres for which she was responsible that day. With a little time on their hands they also tidied the relatives' room, which had been recently made more comfortable with money collected through raffles at the recent autumn fête. Fiona removed a magazine with graphic pictures of a recent motorway pile-up. 'That's hardly suitable reading for distressed relatives,' she remarked.

It was after their coffee break that a domestic crisis erupted in the department.

Mrs Peters, an elderly lady brought in by ambulance

with a suspected fractured neck of femur, was accompanied by her fifteen-year-old granddaughter, who had found her on the floor that morning. She was shocked and chilled and in considerable pain.

'So were you lying there all night, love?' Fiona queried as she and her student helper attended to her immediate needs.

The woman nodded feebly. 'If our Tracey had come home when she should have, I wouldn't have been. Slipped off the step-stool as I was pulling me curtains last night, see. She didn't get 'ome till this morning. Good job I give 'er the key.'

'Yes, I suppose it was.' Fiona cast a puzzled glance towards her student helper as they warmed the patient with blankets and supported her painful limb with sandbags. The youngster outside was just a schoolgirl.

Adrian had already made his preliminary assessment, ordered a pain-killing injection and gone off to report to the consultant.

'There'll be another doctor coming to see you soon, Mrs Peters,' Fiona told her. 'It's pretty certain you've broken your hip, but that can be fixed once you're feeling a little better. I'll go and take a few details from your granddaughter, then she can come and sit with you until the doctors make up their minds what to do.'

The teenager outside sat twisting her hands abjectly. She was dressed in black leggings, tight denim mini-skirt and jacket, and her brown hair sat up in spiky tufts.

'Hello, are you Tracey?' Fiona sat down beside the girl and gave her a friendly smile.

'Yeah! She's going to be OK, ain't she?' the youngster asked breathily.

'She should be. She's had a nasty shake-up, of course. Do you live with her?'

'No, only I stay sometimes, like when I go out with me mates to a disco. It's a better bus service than to our place, but I missed the last one last night.' The explanations came tumbling out. 'Well, I couldn't 'elp it, could I? It must have gone early or something. So I 'ad to go back to me friend's house till this morning.'

'Oh, I see.' Fiona couldn't help feeling sorry for the girl; she was obviously scared out of her wits. 'Well, try not to worry. Your gran's not too bad. Have you told your parents yet?'

'The woman next door—the one who got the ambulance—she said she'd phone me mum.'

As they sat talking Adrian walked along accompanied by Rory, who gave the teenager a smile before entering the grandmother's cubicle.

'He looks nice,' Tracey said. 'Better'n our bloke. Our doctor would crack 'is face if he smiled at yer.'

Fiona gave a soft laugh. 'I'll be back in a moment to let you know what's going to happen,' she said, and she went to join the doctors.

The consultant carried out his examination with his usual quiet courtesy, and, after deciding to admit Mrs Peters to a care assessment ward, to prepare her for the necessary surgery, they moved outside the cubicle to talk.

'Is there a relative here with her?' Rory asked.

'Only the girl sitting over there,' Fiona told him.

He frowned as his eyes followed hers. 'That lass? She looks petrified. What were you telling her?'

'It wasn't what I was telling her. I think she's afraid she may be in trouble when her mother finds out she came home with the milk this morning.'

Their conversation tailed off as a harassed-looking young woman in tight jeans and a purple windcheater burst into the department. Catching sight of the girl, she hurried in her direction and struck her a resounding blow across the face.

'And where was you last night, then?' she demanded. 'What you been up to? I always knew you wasn't to be trusted, you young slag-heap. Just wait till I get you 'ome.'

Her tirade stopped as she suddenly became aware of her audience and the disapproval on their faces. Her gaze swung past them to glimpse Mrs Peters in the cubicle. 'Oh, there you are, Ma,' she said, breathing heavily. 'You don't look too bad, thank Gawd. What she done, Doc?' she appealed to the white-coated Adrian.

It was Rory who answered, and his deep voice held a note of steel. 'Do I understand this lady is your mother?' She nodded, and he went on, 'Mrs Peters has a fractured hip.'

The newcomer rolled her eyes to heaven. 'Jeez! As if I ain't got enough on me plate without this. And she don't help none,' she added with a baleful glare at the teenager. 'Flamin' kids!'

'I would prefer your mother not to be worried any more than necessary,' the consultant told her, but his manner softened a little. 'She'll need an operation, but she'll be going to the ward to rest before that. You may go with her, but before then I need to have some details, if you'd be good enough to come to my office.'

The commotion died down as Rory escorted the woman away. Meanwhile Fiona tried to comfort the tearful Tracey. 'Your mother had a nasty shock too,' she said, 'and worry makes people do and say things they don't always mean, love. So don't take it too much to heart.'

What was said behind closed doors was private

between the consultant and the visitor, but a more chastened person came out to go to the ward with her mother.

When all was quiet Rory came to find Fiona. 'I'd like that family checked out to see if they're on the NAI register,' he said. 'There are three other children, with various fathers, and the lady seemed quite handy with her fists.' He stroked his cheek thoughtfully. 'She also seemed like someone very near the end of her tether.'

'I'll make sure it's looked into,' Fiona promised, making the cubicle ready for the next casualty.

He gave her that direct look which brooked no argument. 'Do it yourself, please. And a.s.a.p.'

She also had been very disturbed by the fracas. 'I will—I will! The first moment I get,' she returned impatiently. 'I'll tie a knot in my hankie.'

The suspicion of a smile relaxed his stern features. 'Tie a knot in your tongue might be more appropriate. But I'm glad you've not lost your sense of humour.'

He returned to his office, and the student still dogging Fiona's footsteps sighed. 'He's gorgeous, isn't he?'

'A gorgeous grouch,' Fiona scowled, but she got down to her appointed task promptly after first clearing it with Sister Bland.

'Oh, go ahead, Fiona,' the sister nodded. 'It's his new policy. He likes people to get involved and see through what they've started.'

In their own locality Fiona drew a blank. The children were not on the non-accidental injury list. She checked with their GP, who said the family was a recent addition to his list, having moved from New Cross, but he had no evidence of violence to the children.

She reported back to Rory, who was not wholly

satisfied. 'Get the Social Services to check with New Cross,' he said.

A few phone calls later and she had the answer. Yes, the family had been on the register in New Cross, but had been lost contact with. They would now be followed up at their present address.

Again Fiona passed on the information she had unearthed, and this time the consultant nodded his approval. 'That was worth your time and trouble, wasn't it, if it saves a child slipping through the net?' he said. 'Thank you, Fiona.'

Relieved at last to have satisfied him, she went to lunch, sharing a table with Bea.

'Gosh, I'd sooner have him on my side than against me,' Fiona declared. 'He doesn't give up easily once he get his teeth into something.'

'No. . .wonder if I could get his support for starting a crèche for nurses' babies? They'd get more of us returning to work if they did.'

'Yes, it must be difficult for you,' Fiona sympathised. 'All I want right now is a nice quiet afternoon without a consultant in sight.'

'You'll be lucky,' Bea scoffed.

Sister Bland buttonholed Fiona immediately on her return. 'Got a job right up your street,' she said. 'There's a five-year-old with a minor cut on his leg. . .it'll need a couple of stitches. . . Kinross doesn't like Steri-Strips. But the child was screaming blue murder even before he was touched. His mother's a bag of nerves too. Anyway, you can handle it.'

'Gee, thanks!' Fiona grinned. 'At least it'll make a change from chasing up the Social Services.'

After checking the child's details on the admission card, she collected her student helper, foreseeing the possible need for assistance. 'But remembering the three Ps, we should manage all right,' she said.

'What are they?' Tina asked.

'Patience, perseverance, and lots of praise.' Fiona led the way to the specially designed area for youngsters, where there were toys and mobiles for their amusement.

In one of the treatment areas a plump little boy sat on a chair alongside his mother, his eyes large with apprehension, his bottom lip tremulous.

'Hello! Are you David?' asked Fiona, her warm smile including both mother and child. She stooped down to his level. 'I've come to have a look at your poor leg so that we can make it better.'

David immediately burst into stormy tears. 'I don't want it made better! I want to go home!'

'Oh, dear! I can't let you go home with a dirty bandage like that. And it's all coming off. You help me unwrap it and let me put on a nice clean one.'

Making sympathetic noises as the mother explained how her son came to be playing with his father's Stanley knife, Fiona was at last able to examine the gash in his calf. 'That's not too bad,' she murmured comfortingly. 'Look, I've got a magic spray here which will take the pain away.'

With Tina holding on to his foot, and after a fair amount of squirming and paroxysms of tears, the required cleansing and stitching was finally accomplished.

Fiona silenced the howling with a lollipop from the stock which they kept especially. She called David a very brave boy and advised the mother that the two stitches could be taken out at her doctor's surgery in a week's time, and waved them thankfully goodbye.

'He wasn't a bit brave,' Tina protested. 'He was a spoiled little horror.'

Fiona grinned. 'A little white lie works wonders. He'll be on an ego trip for the rest of the week.'

The rest of the day continued to be heavy, dominated by child casualties, which made considerable emotional demands on the nurses concerned. Going off duty an hour late after helping Adrian to deal with a schoolgirl who had overdosed on Panadol, Fiona had lost her enthusiasm for her date with Rory that evening. She didn't in the least feel like making the effort to be sociable.

Lois was on a late that day, so there was no one she could open her heart to about the domestic drama just unfolded. Over a solitary coffee in her own flat her head was full of the nightmare existence of the sixteen-year-old girl whom they had needed to make vomit with the aid of ipecac. Abused by her stepfather, her shoulders and arms a mass of bruises, Bridget had been sullen and withdrawn. Had it not been for an alert and sympathetic teacher, who knew what might have become of her? Fiona brooded.

With a determined effort to forget the unpalatable side of life, Fiona ran herself a bath, tipped in a generous helping of bath essence and prepared to make herself presentable for her escort.

What would they talk about? she wondered. In their student days Rory and her brother had been sports-mad alongside their studies. She knew they'd played rugby together, and indulged in the usual student junketing. But their lives had been a whole decade further on than her own. Then she hadn't even started to think about O levels. Apart from their work, would she and Rory have anything in common?

# CHAPTER THREE

Now that the recent rainy spell had passed, the weather was mild and beautiful for mid-October. Fiona pondered for a time over what to wear for her dinner date with Rory, firstly because she was anxious to dispose of this 'little sister' image once and for all, and secondly because she had no idea where he would be taking her. She finally decided on a slimline cherry-red jersey-knit dress as being suitable for anywhere.

Her first-floor living-room window overlooked the wooded front gardens of Sycamore Grange. As eight o'clock drew near she glanced out, awaiting the consultant's arrival. A full moon rode like a great golden orb over the darkening landscape, filling the night with its radiance. A really romantic setting, she thought wistfully, although this was in no way intended to be a romantic liaison. Psyching herself up into being at least good company, she decided there was no point in trying to create an impression; she would just be herself. And despite his standing, Rory was just a guy, with his own highs and lows like everyone else. Although she didn't suppose *he* would be having butterflies at the thought of dining with *her*.

His car crunched on to the gravel drive within a few minutes of eight. Picking up her navy blazer and small leather bag, Fiona ran down to meet him, finding him on the doorstep contemplating the names on the entryphones.

Her pulse bounded at the sight of him, elegant in well-

37

tailored grey suit, a crisp blue shirt enhancing the brilliance of his compelling blue eyes. 'Hi!' she exclaimed over-brightly. 'You found me.'

'Yes, it wasn't difficult.' Walking back towards his car, he eyed her with an appreciative smile. 'You look very charming tonight.'

'Thank you. I thrive on compliments,' she grinned. She climbed into the BMW and settled back comfortably against the beige leather upholstery. 'Where are we going?'

'To Sonning—the White Hart, by the river. Do you know it?' He turned the car in the direction of the picturesque old village.

'Yes, lovely,' she said. 'I've been there before. A pity it's not daylight, though. It's gorgeous by the river. Water is so—restorative, isn't it?' She knew she was chattering, but it was a case of feeling her way.

Rory gave her a sideways glance, looking amused. 'We-ell, that depends where it is, and how much there is of it.'

'Oh, you know what I mean. In a controlled situation, of course,' Fiona put in quickly. 'I know that where you've been, with cyclones and floods and whatever, it's a totally different story.'

'Yes, then it becomes a threat. But I agree with you, the Thames around here can be very soothing.' He paused, then asked, 'Are you in any particular need of being soothed at the moment?'

She laughed lightly. 'No, not at the moment. But I could have done with a bit of peace and tranquillity earlier on today.'

He raised an eyebrow. 'Because of that problem family I asked you to chase up this morning?'

'Good heavens, no, nothing to do with that. This

afternoon there was this. . .' Just in time Fiona stopped
herself from mentioning the sixteen-year-old Bridget's
attempted suicide. Suicide was the last subject she ought
to be talking about where he was concerned.

'Well, go on,' Rory encouraged. 'I like to know about
staff problems.'

'Oh, it was just a heavy sort of day altogether,' she
returned dismissively. 'You know how it is sometimes.
Let's forget work. It'll still be there waiting for us
tomorrow.'

The consultant smiled. 'Too true. And perhaps it's as
well that we don't know what tomorrow will bring.'

They had by now crossed the picturesque many-
arched bridge spanning the river and arrived at the
ancient hostelry in its delightful waterside setting. After
pre-dinner drinks they were shown to a windowside
table in the stylish restaurant. Their seats looked out on
to floodlit flowerbeds and lawns sloping gently down to
the tree-fringed Thames with its moorings for pleasure
craft.

Fiona spent the first few minutes with her chin on her
palm, gazing dreamily out at the pastoral scene. The
veil of mist skimming the surface of the water, and the
harvest moon above, made it seem almost unreal. And
the moment was made all the more poignant by the
magnetism of this man from her distant past; those days
of innocence and happy-ever-afters.

'Why the big sigh?' Rory's deep voice broke through
her thoughts.

Across the flickering flame of the pink candle in its
silver holder she turned starry eyes to his. 'I was just
enjoying the view,' she said.

'The view from where I'm sitting is pretty good too,'
he returned.

She wrinkled her nose at his teasing expression and waited while they were served with the cream of pheasant soup they had ordered. 'Mmm. . .this is delicious,' she said, sipping it appreciatively. 'I'm glad you chose to come here. I wondered if you might be into Indian cuisine after your recent travels.'

'Yes, I am quite partial to it, but I wouldn't have inflicted it on you without querying it first.'

'What brought you home, by the way?' she asked.

'I'd served my time and there was a replacement. Medicine advances so rapidly it doesn't do to lose touch with progress—and McPhail had me lined up to come here.' Rory paused, his unwavering gaze seducing her senses. 'But we're not here to talk about me. I want to know what decided you to embark on this fairly arduous career instead of something less demanding.'

'Like what?' she challenged, endeavouring to ignore his sensual appeal. 'Surely all jobs are as demanding as the amount of effort you care to put into them?'

He smiled wryly. 'Yes—but that doesn't tell me what made you choose nursing.'

'Well, if you *must* know, it was James's idea really,' Fiona admitted. 'He said it would be best for both my mother and me if I branched out on my own. After Dad died we did kind of cling together. James said it was stopping my mother from making her own social contacts. He talked me into training at the Royal Heathside, to keep an eye on me, I guess. I didn't have a vocation as such, but I like human contact, and nursing grew on me. Now I wouldn't want to do anything else.' She grew silent while their main course of traditional roast sirloin was served. 'So that's me, and on reflection it was a good move.'

'How long have you been qualified?'

'Three years. I had to have two goes at my Final,' she confessed. 'A disastrous love-affair threw me off course the first time.'

He shook his dark head and tutted. 'And what's the state of your heart today? I shan't have an indignant boyfriend gunning for me tonight, shall I?'

She chuckled. 'He'd have a job—he's in Florida.' She told him about Craig and that he would be back soon. 'But I don't know where we shall go from there. People's feelings can change in a year.'

His shrewd eyes searched hers. 'Do you mean that yours have?'

'We-ell, let's say the old fires have burned a bit low. I'm keeping my options open for the time being,' she said airily. There was no need to explain to him that, on her part, the fires were long since dead.

'Oh, like that, is it? Hmm!' He continued to keep her under attentive scrutiny before saying, 'Why aren't you a sister by now? I should have thought you were well qualified to handle the job?'

Fiona gave a careless shrug. 'I like the way I am. I prefer dealing with the hands-on side of things to running the show.'

'Or are you just shirking responsibility?'

'No, I'm not,' she retorted indignantly. 'Knowing the situations we're constantly faced with in A and E, I don't see how you can accuse me of that.'

He raised a peaceful hand. 'I only asked.'

She grinned self-consciously. 'To tell the truth, I don't much like giving orders. . .'

'You'd get used to that, and it can be done without being officious. Confidence grows with practice.'

Finishing her meal, Fiona raised her glass to him with a touch of impishness. 'Thank you for those words of wisdom, kind sir. I'll give the matter my serious consideration should the opportunity arise.'

'Opportunities, Miss Rogers, don't arise. They're created by the person looking for them.' Rory's eyes glinted wickedly. 'So that's something else you should give your serious consideration, young lady.'

She cast despairing eyes to the heavens. 'What with my brother, and now you, I'm becoming thoroughly— what's the opposite to henpecked?'

They both laughed, and it occurred to Fiona that, far from being overawed that evening, she was enjoying herself immensely.

'Would you like anything else?' Rory asked as the waiter hovered after removing their plates.

'I'll settle for coffee.' She patted her tummy. 'I'm still recovering from a surfeit of Belgian chocolates my stepfather provided me with.'

'Oh, yes, James said that's where you'd been.' Rory escorted her to the lounge with its subdued wall-lighting, intimate low tables and comfortable damask-covered sofas and chairs. 'Your mother's happy the second time around, is she?'

'She seems to be.' Fiona selected a window alcove. It was approaching ten o'clock now and the night sky was a starry canopy over the sleeping countryside.

Her companion took a chair alongside hers, stretching out, crossing one well-shod foot over the other, his hands resting comfortably in his lap. Like a man at ease with himself and the world, she thought.

'Only seems to be?' he asked, with that endearing half-smile and slightly raised eyebrow.

'Well, *is*, then. Only no one knows for sure how anyone else feels, do they? I don't think there'll ever be anyone quite like my father. I know she still thinks of him.'

His voice was gentle. 'Of course she does. You don't stop loving people when they die.'

She caught her bottom lip between her teeth for a moment, to control the tremble. 'I know. Life goes on, doesn't it? She's happy in a different way, I suppose. My problem is, I'm not part of her life any more.'

He laid a hand over hers, giving it a comforting squeeze. 'You'll always be part of her life. You're her child.'

The coffee came. She poured it and pushed his across, raising a smile. 'That's quite enough about me. Do you have parents still living?'

'Just my mother—a very strong-minded lady. She's a GP in Edinburgh, and we get on better with a few miles between us.'

Fiona nibbled at the chocolate mint which came with the coffee. 'Sounds like *two* strong-minded people,' she murmured.

He laughed. 'You may be right. She did, after all, raise me single-handed. My father went off with someone else when I was a toddler.'

'Oh! That must have been really tough. She needed to be strong, didn't she?' Fiona countered.

He nodded in agreement, but he didn't enlarge on the subject. For a time they were both silent. She assumed that he too was back in the past. '*You don't stop loving people when they die*', he had said—which surely, for him, meant the girl he had loved. Poor Rory, she thought. With medical skills at his fingertips, and he still could do nothing to help her.

Her gaze wandered idly around the comfortable coffee lounge where groups of people sat relaxing after their meal. There was an average mix of ages; family parties and couples both young and old. Across the room sat a pleasant-looking elderly pair, both solidly built, but it was the man who caught her particular attention.

His plump, agreeable face was a little too flushed and he had a hand out to his companion while waiting for some kind of tablet which she was unwrapping for him. An indigestion tablet, Fiona concluded absently. But alarm bells rang in her head when the man suddenly levered himself out of his chair, clutching at his chest. Sweat glistened on his forehead, his lips were blue, and with his face beginning to darken in colour he began stumbling off in the direction of the toilets.

It was out of the consultant's line of vision, but Fiona's concerned expression made him ask what was the matter.

She half rose from her chair. 'Rory, I think that man's in trouble. Perhaps you should—— Oh, God!'

His gaze following hers, they witnessed the man's collapse on to the ruby-rich carpet, where he writhed and panted in obvious distress.

His wife's hand flew to her mouth. With a frightened squeal she ran to his side. 'Oh—oh, dear! *Please*. . .can someone help?' she appealed frantically.

Even before she had finished speaking Rory was out of his chair, recognising the need for prompt medical aid. Handing his car keys to Fiona as he went, he murmured, 'My emergency bag. . .it's in the boot. As fast as you can.'

Having dealt with enough coronary problems to know how every moment was vital, she needed no urging to hurry. While Rory briefly introduced himself and dropped to his knees beside the unfortunate diner she sped to the car park, returning to bring him his bag containing the life-saving drugs he carried for such emergencies.

The victim was still fully conscious and in great pain, but by this time an agitated waiter had found a screen to shield him from the public eye and the hum of concerned voices. Rory had also made his assessment and sent for an ambulance.

'Ah, thank you,' he murmured, opening the bag Fiona had brought. 'Mr Webb, I'm going to give you a couple of injections which should help matters until we get you to hospital.'

His clothing had already been loosened and Fiona cushioned the man's head on her knees while the doctor administered adrenalin and atropine. She then stayed with him while Rory sought to comfort the distraught Mrs Webb.

The woman was biting back her tears and twisting her rings anxiously. 'I-it's his birthday,' she said. 'His seventieth. H-he is going to be all right, isn't he, doctor?'

'He's quite ill, Mrs Webb,' Rory warned. 'The injections I've given will have saved valuable time, I hope. Once he's in hospital they'll be able to make the right tests and decide on a proper course of treatment.' He paused and gave her a kindly smile. 'It's lucky my friend and I were here.'

'Oh, yes, it was. I'm so grateful.' With a heavy sigh the woman looked down at Fiona, still in her caring role beside the casualty. 'I'm so sorry if it's spoiled your evening.'

'Not at all. The lady is a nurse. . .she understands.'

To the immense relief of everyone the ambulance arrived, and after giving the paramedics details of the drugs he had given Rory handed the patient over to their care.

It was thought best that his wife should follow in their own car. After seeing her to the car park and making sure there was nothing further they could do for her, Fiona and Rory returned to the hotel.

'I do hope he makes it. It'll be awful if he—peters out before she gets there,' Fiona said.

'I don't think that will happen, but if it does it'll be less harrowing than to have it happen here, for instance. There was a history of angina, she told me.'

Back in the coffee lounge the hotel manager came to thank them for their efforts, offering to replace their coffee, which was now cold.

Rory glanced at Fiona, who shook her head, feeling conspicuous after their involvement. 'No, thanks. I think we should be going.'

While he settled the account she collected her jacket and freshened up in the cloakroom. Then they went out into the refreshing night air and his arm seemed to slip quite naturally around her shoulders. The intimate contact sent an exquisite sensation coursing through every inch of her.

Glancing up into his captivating face, she asked, 'Do you ever get an evening out without interruption?'

'It has been known.' He smoothed back his thick dark hair with an air of playful resignation. 'Luckily for me it's the cardiac boys who'll have to cope tonight.' Reaching the car, he paused to open the doors, and when they were seated he turned to give her his full attention. 'Now what? We can't finish the evening on a note like this. Coffee at your place or mine?'

Fiona gave a light sigh. 'All the windows have eyes in Sycamore Grange. If I take you back there the hospital corridors will be buzzing in no time.'

He chuckled, an infectious sound which made her

bones feel weak. 'Mine it'll have to be, then. I'm renting Ian McPhail's place at Caversham for the time being. Is that far enough from the madding crowd for you?'

'Yes, fine.' She drew a long breath to steady her nerves. 'Right, let's go.'

The leisurely drive back through the dark countryside until they reached the exclusive riverside apartment block on the outskirts of the town had Fiona in an odd frame of mind. She was intrigued by the prospect of seeing Rory in his home environment, yet still caught up in the drama of the evening, unable to forget the anguished features of the woman whose husband had collapsed.

'Stop brooding now and talk to me,' Rory ordered with a sudden intuitive smile.

She nibbled her thumbnail for a moment. 'I was really just thinking what a strange evening it's been.'

'Mmm, you're right there. If only all my dinner dates were as capable in a crisis. Well done, lass!'

'For goodness' sake, my only contribution was a bit of t.l.c.,' she retorted. 'Don't be so damn patronising.'

'No patronage intended,' he said, trying to look contrite. 'My trouble is, I'm still having to come to terms with the fact that my friend's kid sister has grown into an attractive young woman.'

She threw him a dark look, then dissolved into laughter. 'Oh, belt up!'

'That's better.' He grinned at her. 'And I was glad to have you along, honestly.'

Slowing the car, he swung into the grounds of the stylish flats, parking in his reserved garage space. 'It'll only be instant coffee,' he warned, 'but accompanied by some pukka music on my new CD player—if you behave yourself, or some grainy old LPs on McPhail's old music centre if you don't.'

He was merely being facetious, she decided, and made no reply.

A swift silver lift carried them up to his rooms on the second floor. Switching on a number of lights, he showed her into his living-room. 'Make yourself at home,' he said, removing his own jacket and loosening his tie. 'Come and see my newest toy. . .' He walked over to a cabinet housing a compact disc player and took out one of the small iridescent silver discs.

She went to join him, watching as he tilted it this way and that and the colours blended. 'Isn't it amazing?' Rory said. 'Laser sound all neatly tucked up in there. Laser light has so many applications, especially in the world of medicine. It's phenomenal.'

He put the disc into the player and the glorious sounds of a Mozart symphony began to fill the room. Warming to what was obviously a personal interest, he went on to talk about the way laser techniques were changing the face of medicine. Fiona could have listened to his fascinating voice all night, but he suddenly stopped and laughed. 'I'd better put on the kettle. I invited you for coffee, not a lecture.'

Sinking into one of the deep fawn leather armchairs, she felt seduced by the music while she waited his return. Her gaze wandered round the essentially male room. Everything was functional, no pot plants or ornaments as such. But there were two photographs on the mantel-piece—one a studio portrait of a middle-aged woman, who she assumed might be his mother, and the other of a beaming-faced Indian boy of about ten years.

'One of your patients?' she asked, nodding towards the boy when Rory came back with the drinks.

'Yes, we gave him a new leg. One of his own got severed when some brigands attacked his village.'

Fiona smiled. 'He looks a nice kid. I bet that made you feel good.'

'Yes, he was one of our success stories.' Rory gazed at the photograph, remembering. 'Some of the time you felt helpless in the face of poverty and ignorance, and the climate, and the flies. But children like Tariq more than made up for it.'

She drank some coffee. 'How about as he grows—will he be able to get the right replacements?'

'I hope so. He's an orphan. He's at a mission school; the staff there should look after him.' The doctor paused. 'People here don't realise how fortunate they are, having——'

'Oh, yes, they do,' Fiona interrupted. 'The majority do, anyway. There's bound to be the odd grumbler wherever you are.'

He stroked his chin and gave her a wry grin. 'Fair enough, but I can't help thinking of what might be achieved out there with more education, more money and better facilities.' He changed the subject, saying, 'By the way, your brother tells me he and Deborah are planning to marry.'

'Yes, that's great, isn't it? They've been together six years, and if they don't know by now that they're right for each other they never will.'

'I couldn't have put it better myself. So you'd like to see it all nice and legal, would you?'

'If that's what they want, yes. I don't think they should get married just to please other people. . .' She paused, beginning to feel self-conscious under his direct blue gaze. 'But I mean, if they want to start a family, I think babies have the right to a conventional beginning, don't you?'

He looked slightly amused to find her blushing. 'Is that the reason for this wedding?'

'How should I know?' she said. 'That's their business.'

'Well, when they decide on a date, maybe we could travel together.'

'Mmm, maybe we could.'

The music had finished and he jumped up. 'Do you feel like dancing? I could put on one of McPhail's LPs if you do.'

She would have loved to dance, for the sheer delight of having him hold her. But for that very reason she decided it best not to. 'Not tonight,' she said, 'I really ought to be going.'

He didn't attempt to persuade her otherwise. Picking up her jacket, he helped her into it, afterwards letting his strong hands slide down her arms. 'Do you remember how I could lift you up by your elbows when you were a little girl?' he said.

Of course she did! She could well remember how he had raised her effortlessly high in the air. 'That's something you couldn't do now,' she laughed.

'Betcha! Want a demonstration?'

She shook her head. 'No, thanks. We can do without a show of strength to boost your ego.'

'Oh, come on. You wouldn't deprive a six-foot-two weakling of his ego trip,' he pleaded. 'Tuck your elbows in.'

With a resigned sigh and a pounding heart she did as he asked. He raised her on high, looking up at her with a self-satisfied grin. 'You lose your bet, lady. What were the stakes?'

'There wasn't a bet. And you can let me down now.'

He allowed her body to slide enticingly past his, holding it level for a moment as their faces drew abreast. There was barely an inch between them, and she could feel the warmth of his skin and sense the devilment in his curving mouth. 'That's one you owe me, then,' he murmured before letting her feet touch the ground.

She wrinkled her nose at him. 'OK, so you proved your point. Men will be boys, I suppose.'

The drive back to her own flat was only remarkable for its silence. Rory seemed disinclined for chitchat and Fiona was still recovering her senses after being unceremoniously raised on high. The physical contact was even more electrifying than she had thought possible. No other man had excited her so much. Which was nothing less than disastrous, when he had as good as admitted that he was still in love with the girl who had died.

He walked with her as far as the doorstep. 'Thank you, Fiona, for a very pleasant evening. Despite that hiccup in the middle of it, I enjoyed renewing our acquaintance.'

'Me too,' she said. 'I can't help wondering how our casualty is getting on, though. It would be nice to think we helped to avert disaster.'

Rory took out a pocketbook and pen. 'Give me your phone number and I'll let you know. I intended going on to the hospital to make enquiries.'

'You did? Oh, great.'

He wrote down the number she gave him. 'I'll be in touch,' he promised. 'Well, goodnight, and thanks again for your company.' He raised her hand to his lips, patted her briefly on the shoulder and was gone.

Back in her own flat Fiona waited for his call, wondering if he really would ring or get involved with other things. But within half an hour he came on with the gratifying news that Mr Webb had been admitted to ICU and was holding his own.

'So you can sleep with an easy mind now,' he said. 'Pleasant dreams, Fiona.'

But how could she sleep when her head was full of him? She relived the thrill of his strong body, warm against hers in that show of masculinity. It was a seductive action, even if he hadn't meant it to be. And she didn't suppose he had, since he had only gone as far as kissing her hand on seeing her to the doorstep.

So that was it, she thought, turning her pillow and thumping it. They had more or less resumed the relationship where they had left off eleven years ago. She was *still* his friend's kid sister—even if she had wondered whether there might be a spark of something waiting to flare into life if he would let it.

But she had given him no encouragement, on account of the difference in their status. And Rory was a man of strong control as well as physical strength. In any case, twenty-four-year-old nurses probably didn't enter into his scheme of things. And because she was James's sister he wouldn't fool around with her, would he? He had certainly been a bit flirtatious, though.

Fiona sighed heavily. He was without doubt the most exciting man she had ever met, arousing the same earthy feelings in her that he had awakened in her youth. But he was simply out of her orbit, much though she wished it could be otherwise. Maintaining good working relationships was the best she could hope for. She would have to settle for that.

# CHAPTER FOUR

SISTER BLAND was about to go off for her long weekend the following Friday lunchtime when she sprang her surprise to the oncoming staff.

'I'll be leaving here at the end of November,' she told them. 'I've landed a job as nursing officer at St Martin's in London.'

There were cries of genuine delight at her success, coupled with regret at her departure. Fiona spoke for them all when she exclaimed, 'Oh, congrats, Molly! That's terrific. But we shall miss you.'

'Well, I'm not a hundred per cent chuffed at the thought of going,' the sister confessed, 'but there's no prospect of promotion for me here, with the present hierarchy well and truly dug in. Anyway,' she gave a resigned smile, 'it's a good thing to have a change of scene sometimes. Stops you getting stale.'

She went off duty then, leaving Fiona in charge as senior nurse and all of them to mull over the news, in between attending to the ever-changing flow of patients.

They were quite well staffed until the early shift would depart at four-thirty, and during a break for tea for the late shift speculation continued.

'I wonder who'll get her job?' Aileen, a recent addition to the department, had a gleam in her kohl-rimmed eyes. 'It'll have to be advertised, of course, but they're bound to favour an in-house applicant, aren't they? I may as well have a try for it myself.'

Bea and Tony—a newish male staff nurse—

53

exchanged meaningful glances. Aileen's pushy manner did not go down too well with the rest of them.

'Anyone's entitled to apply, given the right qualifications,' Bea said. 'As I'm a part-timer, it's not open to me and I wouldn't want it. What about you, Fiona? You could do it.'

Sipping her tea, Fiona was thoughtful. She wondered if Rory had known about this when he'd asked her why she wasn't a sister. The higher grading and extra cash was certainly attractive, and it was time she began to consider the next step in her career. The trouble was, promotion always made a difference to relationships; it was that which bothered her, not the responsibility. Exercising authority could be difficult, especially with some of the younger staff nurses, some of whom were inclined to think they had nothing to learn.

'I don't know,' she hesitated. 'It might be better to start as a sister somewhere else.'

'Oh, don't you leave too!' Rosemary wailed. 'Better the devil you know than the devil you don't.'

Fiona laughed. 'Gee, thanks! Is that meant to be a compliment?'

The bleeper in her pocket sounded and she went back to the office to take the call from the ambulance station, going along to the casualty officer afterwards to alert him of the forthcoming road traffic accident victim.

'Adrian, we're to expect an RTA in fifteen minutes. Twenty-four-year-old male with displaced compound fractures of tib and fib. His name's Tom Skinner—knocked off his motorbike by an oncoming car. Is Rory still around?'

'Should be,' Adrian returned. 'He was doing an arthroscopy earlier this afternoon.' He lifted his telephone. 'I'll give him a buzz.'

'OK—and I'll send Aileen and Rosemary to meet the ambulance.' Fiona went back to the coffee-room to advise the two nurses. 'Make sure you take a Siemen's trolley, Aileen. It's a compound injury.'

Aileen huffed a bit and tossed her blonde-streaked head as she made for the door. 'You're not slow getting into practice for giving your orders!' she said. 'Come on, then, Rosemary.'

Fiona spread her hands in a helpless gesture when the two girls had left. 'What did I say? See what I mean about having to give directions to people you've worked alongside with.'

'Oh, take no notice of her. Nobody can tell Aileen anything,' Tony declared.

At about the same time as the expected casualty arrived, Fiona's attention was claimed elsewhere by a young mother who rushed up to her in a state of panic, her six-month-old baby girl in her arms.

'Please help me. . .she's had some kind of fit.' The girl was half crying as she thrust the infant towards Fiona. 'Sh-she'd been fine all day, then as I was about to give her a feed she suddenly went all stiff, and then she started twitching. What do you think it can be, Nurse?' she appealed, wringing her hands.

It took only one glance at the well-wrapped infant in her arms for Fiona to realise that the baby was very ill. She was extremely pale, eyes wide and unblinking, and apart from the odd twitching movement she seemed scarcely alive.

'I would think she's had a convulsion,' Fiona said, keeping her voice calm. 'It's not uncommon with babies of this age.' She led the way to a cubicle. 'Let's have a look at her and take her temperature. Perhaps she's starting a cold.'

Upon undressing the child she found her beautifully cared for and well nourished—but her rectal temperature was 40 C. 'Mmm, that's much too high,' she said, wrapping her up in a cotton blanket. 'I'll get a doctor to see her.'

With Adrian otherwise occupied, Fiona took it upon herself to call down the paediatrician with all possible speed.

Dr Patrick Green came at once, recognising the urgency in her request. He was a lively but gentle dark-eyed Irishman who managed to be both calm and reassuring while not minimising the gravity of the baby's condition. Working with unhurried efficiency, he attached her to a monitor, administered oxygen, put up an IV dextrose-saline drip and called for a portable chest X-ray. The X-ray plates revealed what he suspected—signs of pneumonia.

'We shall need to admit Georgina for a few days, Mrs Longman,' he told the anxious young mother. 'Your baby is quite ill. . .but I've seen worse, my dear, and we've a dedicated bunch of nurses upstairs to look after her.' He gave an encouraging smile as the girl's bottom lip trembled. 'You'll be able to stay in with her, if that's convenient for you.'

'Oh, my goodness! She seemed perfectly all right this morning. I don't know how this could have happened,' the girl despaired.

'Nothing to blame yourself for—you did all the right things. These infections can blow up in no time.' With a few private instructions to Fiona, the doctor then left to arrange for the admission.

Having completed the appropriate forms, Fiona

entrusted Bea with the task of taking baby and mother to the paediatric intensive care ward.

Despite having had to keep her own emotions well under control, Fiona experienced a sense of satisfaction at a crisis well handled. Her step was buoyant as she went to make a tour of the department to ensure that no other urgent cases were being neglected. It was then that Rory Kinross came to find her.

'I'd like a word, please,' he said.

There was a chill in his voice which seemed to bode trouble. She had seen little of him since the previous week, and this was certainly not how she had imagined their next contact would be. She had pictured at least a harmonious relationship. Yet here he was, his manner almost brusque.

'Yes?' she returned, casting about for some misdemeanour on her part.

Of necessity she followed him as he started walking back towards the examination cubicle where Tom Skinner—the accident victim—was still being assessed.

Pausing just outside the curtains, Rory went on in quiet tones, 'I've just been called to see this patient with compound fractures of the lower leg, and I find him on a commonplace trolley.' His direct blue gaze was accusing, his manner scathing. 'Why on earth, when you have every sophisticated appliance to hand, including trolleys with X-ray suitability, did you not use one? Now this poor lad has to be moved yet again before he can be X-rayed. Please make sure that this doesn't occur in future when you happen to be in charge.'

With that he walked back into the cubicle, leaving her wide-eyed, open-mouthed and furious. As he had swished back the curtains she caught a glimpse of Aileen, who glanced away rather quickly on the pretext of assisting Adrian, who was taking blood for cross-matching.

For a moment Fiona was transfixed, her cheeks flushed with indignation, tears stinging her eyes. She brushed them angrily away, taking deep breaths to regain control before returning to her work. As far as Rory was concerned the matter was closed, and there was nothing she could do about it. She must certainly not risk giving him grounds for further complaint. Resolutely she went back to the waiting area to make sure that there was no one else in need of life-saving treatment. Back in the office she sought to put the distressing episode behind her by concentrating on some necessary paperwork.

Presently, returning from Paediatrics, Bea came to join her. 'That was a lovely baby,' she said. 'Her mum was scared to death in case it might have been the start of epilepsy. So I tried to explain about convulsions often being symptomatic of rapid rises in temperature. But they can be frightening, can't they?' She paused, suddenly noticing Fiona's unusually downcast attitude. 'What's biting you?'

Injured feelings resurfacing, it was a relief to Fiona to explain what had happened.

'You heard me tell Aileen to take a Siemen's trolley for that RTA, didn't you? Well, it seems she didn't, and Kinross read *me* the riot act. Perhaps I should have checked up on her after that little show of pique in the coffee-room. But we were involved with baby Georgina at the time, and if you can't trust your trained staff to do the right thing—well. . .'

The older girl raised her eyebrows. 'Didn't you tell him you'd given instructions?'

'He didn't give me the chance, the pompous twit. And

if I had it would probably have sounded feeble, like me trying to pass the buck.'

'Well, Aileen shouldn't have needed telling, in any case. You've got to watch your back with that one,' Bea declared with a short laugh. 'It's tough at the top, kid, but don't let it put you off.'

'No, I jolly well won't after this.'

'Will you tackle her about it?'

'I shan't drag it up unless she says something to me. I can't be bothered.' Fiona stretched her arms above her head as though to push away the problem. 'But I'll make damn sure there's not a next time!'

Bea grinned. 'All water under the bridge. It'll probably be forgotten by the time you next see your pompous twit.' She looked a her fob-watch. 'And it's time I was away. Can't wait to get back to my own little pet. Seeing that other poor mite made me want to dash home and check on my own. See you, Fiona.'

Some time later a harassed middle-aged woman arrived in the department and was directed to Fiona after enquiring at the desk.

'I'm Tom Skinner's mother,' she said, her cheeks pink with hurrying. 'I understand he was brought here. I was at work, but I came as soon as the police got through to me. H-how is he. . .may I see him?'

By this time the casualty had been fully X-rayed and transferred to the orthopaedic floor to await reduction of his fractures.

'Yes, I'm sure you can,' Fiona returned with a pleasant smile. 'He's as comfortable as can be expected for the time being. There's considerable damage to his leg, I'm afraid, but no other injuries as far as the doctors could tell. We've transferred him to Paget Ward on the second floor. If you'd like to go up I'm sure he'll be very glad to see you.'

The mother took out a handkerchief, struggling against tears. 'W-would it be possible to see one of the doctors? I'd like to know how he's going to be. I mean, how long. . .' She blew her nose.

Fiona put a comforting arm around her shoulders. 'I think the consultant who's dealing with him is still somewhere about. Sit down for a moment and I'll try and find him for you.'

Rory was where she had thought him to be—in the doctors' office, completing his case-notes. When she knocked and opened the door he glanced up.

'Fiona, what can I do for you?' he asked, all trace of his former displeasure gone.

'Mr Skinner's mother has just arrived and would like to see you,' she replied levelly.

'Fine.' He bent his classic head and resumed his writing. 'Bring her along, will you?'

She did as he asked, and saw Rory rise to greet the woman as she left them together. In due time Mrs Skinner emerged, looking a little more cheerful.

'Thanks, love,' she said, looking in on Fiona before going to see her son. 'Now I know Tom's not about to lose his leg or anything dreadful like that, I shan't blub all over him when I see him. Motorbikes!' she despaired, rolling her eyes. 'I never wanted him to have one. That doctor's a nice fellow, isn't he?'

It was not exactly Fiona's sentiment at the time, but she nodded in agreement. 'Your son's in good hands, Mrs Skinner,' she said.

The evening passed with a steady flow of minor injuries and the usual cuts and bruises typical of Friday-night pub brawls. At nine-thirty Fiona was not sorry to hand over to the night staff after what had been a trying day. Taking off her cap in the staff-room, she found herself unexpectedly alone with Aileen. At first neither girl spoke, then Aileen began, with a degree of embarrassment,

'Er—Fiona, about that trolley business. Sorry if it put you on the spot, but I think Kinross went over the top, reacting the way he did. For Pete's sake, at my last hospital we only ever used specialist trolleys for fractured femurs or spinal injuries.'

Changing her white duty shoes for brown suede fashion boots, Fiona finished what she was doing before standing up and giving the other girl her attention. 'Here we use them whenever necessary to save patients from extra handling,' she said. 'And I did mention it to you.'

'Yeah, I remember something about it, but there wasn't one handy, and the ambulance had arrived,' Aileen went on lamely. 'Er—what did you say to Kinross?'

'Your name wasn't mentioned, if that's what you want to know,' Fiona replied. 'You boobed, but let's forget it.'

The other girl laughed. 'Well, a lot of fuss about nothing, if you ask me. Gosh, Kinross doesn't often flip his lid, but when he does, watch out!' She stuffed her cap into her holdall and zipped up her weatherproof jacket. 'Well, I'm off. Cheerio!'

'Goodnight, Aileen.' Fiona made an effort to be civil. They had to work together, after all. In any case, she had a more pressing matter on her mind.

Much as she adored working in A and E, the disadvantage was that patients came and went, and much of the time you never knew how they had fared after passing on into other hands, unless you made a special effort to find out. There was no time to build up relationships as when working on a ward.

It was now over a week since she had dined with Rory and they had come to the rescue of Mr Wells, the heart-attack victim at the White Hart. Fiona had enquired about him on meeting the sister of Coronary Care in the canteen the previous day.

'He's fine, and a dear old chap,' the sister had told her. 'Come up and see him whenever you like. He's probably for discharge in a few days.'

She had hesitated to intrude during normal visiting hours, but this, she thought, would be as good a time as any to pop in for five minutes.

After first clearing her visit with the night nurse in charge, Fiona found Mr Wells just wandering back from the bathroom in his dressing-gown.

'Hello, my dear!' he greeted her in delight. 'How lovely to see you, and sweet of you to take the trouble.'

She perched on the chair by his bed. 'And it's great to see you looking so perky. What did they find out about you?'

'Oh, it was some sort of thrombus, they said. I've had dozens of tests and they've put me on those things they call clotbusters. I'm not going to need surgery—at least for the present, I'm glad to say.'

'That's wonderful.' She beamed at him. 'It was a bit scary that night at the restaurant, wasn't it?'

'You can say that again!' Mr Wells cast his eyes heavenwards. 'I've never felt so terrible. I thought I was a goner. And I might have been had you and the doctor not turned up trumps. You know,' he went on confiden-tially, 'during dinner my wife and I had been saying what a nice couple you made. Are you and he. . .? If you'll forgive my curiosity.'

She smiled and shook her head. 'No, Rory's just a family friend.'

'Oh! You looked so happy together that night, although I can see he must be a good few years older. My wife will be disappointed—she's an incurable romantic. We've no children, you see. She would have loved a daughter like you to plan a wedding for.'

'So think of all the money you saved,' Fiona said jokingly.

He made a regretful face. 'All the money in the world couldn't give her what she wanted. There was no such thing as this IVF programming in our young days.'

'Well, even that can often be like chasing an expensive pipe-dream,' Fiona pointed out gently. 'I expect you've been able to do other things instead.'

'Yes, we've had a good life together. Correction, still have, thanks to all you clever people in the medical profession.'

'Not forgetting the backroom boys and their wonder drugs,' Fiona put in, seeing two of the ward nurses about to dispense the ten p.m. medications. 'I mustn't outstay my welcome. Give my best wishes to your wife, Mr Wells, and take good care of yourself.'

'Thank you again for coming.' He kissed her soft cheek. 'I shall never forget your pretty face.'

In good spirits she left the ward, heartened at his satisfactory outcome. But her heart skipped a beat when she looked along the corridor and saw the stalwart figure of Rory approaching. And to reach the stairs she had no option but to pass him.

'Hello!' He raised his dark eyebrows as she drew closer. 'What are you doing on this floor?'

'I came up to see Mr Wells,' she explained, her voice

amazingly steady considering the rumpus inside her. 'I'd heard he'd be leaving soon.'

'Oh! That's where I was bound, but I'll leave it for now as you've just been.' He turned and fell into step beside her, hands in the pockets of his stylish grey suit. 'It was nice of you to take the trouble.'

'Not really. I'm just a naturally curious sort of person. Anyway, you like people to take a continuing interest in patients, don't you?'

The flippancy in her manner was not lost on him and he gave her a sideways judicial glance. 'Yes, I do. But I don't expect people to go out of their way, and in their own time.'

They had by now reached the end of the corridor and come to the staircase. 'I can please myself what I do in my own time,' she returned crisply.

They descended in silence together, but on reaching the bottom Rory pulled her to one side when she would have gone marching on. 'Now,' he said, with a show of patience, 'what's wrong?'

She looked up at him, her hazel eyes flashing angrily. 'You can't treat people like dirt one minute and come on all sweetness and light the next and expect to resume normal relations.'

At a loss for a moment, he ran a hand over his dark hair, then his frown cleared and he laughed. 'So that's what this is all about. Look, Effie, if anyone needs their hand slapped, then I slap it. Personalities make no difference. Where the well-being of patients is concerned I let no one get away with sloppiness. Outside of work, though, we're you and me, and we can be friends. All right?'

'No, not all right. That's the second time you've wronged me. You'd be advised to make sure of your facts before you start making accusations. And that's my last word on the matter. Goodnight.' With a toss of her fair head and chin in the air Fiona began walking away towards the car park.

He continued to keep pace with her as they went out into the night, a bedevilling smile tilting the corners of his mouth. 'In that case, my humble apologies. I stand corrected. Can we now call a truce?'

'If you promise to get off my back.'

'It's only because I want you to be the best.'

'I am the best. Only you're too. . .too high-handed and self-opinionated to see it.'

They paused on reaching her car, where he put on a mock-solemn face and held out his own hand for punishment. 'There you are, give me what I deserve.'

She accepted the challenge and slapped it, but he caught her hand tightly in his, grinning provocatively. 'Oh, don't be such an ass,' she murmured, unable to keep from smiling back.

He lifted the hand to his lips before letting it go. 'I've got a new CD. How about coming back with me to hear it? We could pick up a pizza on the way.'

She would have loved to do just that now they had cleared the air, but pride would not let her be so easily won over. 'Thanks, but it's far too late, and I'm on an early tomorrow. Some other time, maybe.'

'There might not be another time. Now is the only time you can depend on.'

Trying to think up a suitable reply to that, Fiona had a sudden memory of this girl of his—the one who had ended her own life. There had not been another time for either of them after that. Fiona's manner softened. 'I really am quite tired, Rory. I wouldn't be good company,' she said with a quiet smile.

He studied her critically for a long moment, his powerful presence running rings around her will-power. 'OK, I'll let you off this time,' he said at last. 'Away to bed with you.'

She stepped into her car and drove off, making a mess of the gears as her pulses hammered.

He watched her go before making for his own parking space. And for once his normally discerning blue eyes wore a bemused, faraway expression.

Back at her flat Fiona collected some post from her pigeonhole before going upstairs. Lois, she remembered, had gone home for the weekend, so there would be no girl-talk that night. In a way, being in thoughtful mood, she was rather glad. That brief but emotive encounter with Rory had left her with much to think about. It was disturbing the way his slightest touch could electrify her. She wondered if he knew.

After discarding her uniform for housecoat and slippers, she made coffee and a tuna sandwich, thinking wistfully of the pizza she might have shared with Rory. Then, relaxing on the sofa, she opened her mail while she ate.

There was the usual chatty note from her mother, and an engagement party invitation from her brother—on the back of which James had scrawled, 'Why not drive up with Rory? We can give you both a bed for the night.' It was an intriguing suggestion, but whether wise from her point of view was another matter.

She laid the invitation aside to open her last letter. It was from Craig, giving her details of his flight home in early November, hoping she'd be able to meet him at Heathrow. Pulling her diary from her shoulderbag, she was intent on tying up dates and days off when her telephone rang.

'Rory!' his vibrant voice announced when she picked up the receiver. 'Listen! Can you hear that?'

Rich orchestral sounds came faintly to her ear. 'Yes,' she said, 'sounds brilliant.'

'Just to let you know what you're missing, although that isn't really why I rang. Have you had what I had through the post?'

She smiled to herself. 'How would I know unless you tell me what it is?'

'An invitation to an engagement party.'

'Oh, yes, mine has come too.'

'I shall be off that weekend,' Rory went on. 'We could travel together. Unless, of course, you have other plans?'

Her chest suddenly felt tight. 'Oh!' she murmured, and swallowed. 'I've hardly had time to think about it yet. Thanks for the offer. Can I let you know later?'

'OK. Hope I didn't disturb your beauty sleep. Not that you need any. . .'

'Oh, come on,' she laughed. 'You can forget the flowery speeches. I'm just your pal's kid sister, remember?'

'Yes, we're almost family, aren't we?' he returned cheerfully. 'We can be comfortable together, which is nice.'

When they had said goodbye she sat and pondered on the idea of being with him alone on a two-hour drive to London. It had been bad enough fighting back her sensual reactions on the few times they had been in contact. At the party itself there should be no problem, with a host of other visitors to talk to. But then there would be the return journey after the romantic occasion. It was hardly a recipe for keeping emotions in check.

Of course, she could always make the excuse of looking up old friends and travel back by train. That seemed like a reasonable idea. Pushing the matter to one side for the moment, she tried to concentrate on Craig's letter.

Although she had long since given up all thoughts of Craig as a lover, she had enjoyed their correspondence. It had become more like having a pen-pal, exchanging news and views on their differing lifestyles. But she had never committed to paper her change of heart, excusing herself on the grounds that it would be better said face to face, when she saw him again. With the meeting imminent, she now wondered whether that had been wise, or fair, and decided that perhaps she should give him some warning.

Searching out her airmail pad, she sat at her desk and began to write. Usually she had no problem finding things to say, but tonight her thoughts would not flow from pen to paper. Rory's fascinating face kept intruding. Don't be an idiot! she told herself impatiently. He's just a collection of sinew and muscle rather too attractively packaged.

She chewed the end of her pen as the attractive package continued to plague her—eloquent dark eyebrows, extremely kissable mouth, purposeful jawline, and those magnetic blue eyes.

And all he saw in her was a kind of adopted sister, compensating for the family he didn't have. Oh, Rory!

For the time being she had to give up on her letter. Trying to concentrate was hopeless.

# CHAPTER FIVE

IT WAS re-reading Craig's letter the following morning that helped Fiona to finalise her plans. After a night's sleep her thoughts were clearer. Craig was due to arrive back in England the day before her brother's engagement party. That would work out nicely, since she was to be in London that weekend anyway. With Craig's flight scheduled to touch down at eight-thirty a.m., she decided to travel to Hampstead the night before. That would rule out driving there with Rory and give her the perfect excuse to make her own arrangements without causing offence.

Going in to work that morning, she felt really light of heart. All she need now do was fix her off-duty accordingly and tell Rory at the first convenient moment.

At seven-thirty that Saturday morning the department was empty, with no overflow from the previous night. Fiona was assigned to the Resus area together with new staff nurse, Shirley Campbell, a cheerful West Indian girl. After replenishing stocks and cleaning equipment and surfaces, the two nurses joined the rest of the staff gathered for a coffee break before the arrival of patients.

The coffee-room was buzzing with talk of the party to be held on Mallard's Island the following weekend for Martin Davis, a charge nurse on the orthopaedic floor who was leaving to take a course leading to Nurse Tutor. Martin had formerly worked in A and E and had been well liked by all. This was going to be a popular occasion. Molly Bland had an enormous card there for everyone to sign to accompany the clock-radio for which they had collected.

'Where's this place—Mallard's Island?' Shirley asked.

'It's a floating pub on the river with a large room upstairs for private parties. Super atmosphere,' Fiona told her. 'We often use if for things like this.'

The sister's emergency bleeper sounded. She went off to answer it, returning in a few moments to ask Fiona and Shirley to meet an incoming casualty.

'It's a fifteen-year-old girl, kicked in the face by her horse,' Molly explained. 'She wasn't KO'd, but she's terribly hysterical. We're in the hands of Dr Crewe, I'm afraid. Mr Kinross hasn't arrived yet, although he's expected. And Adrian's gone for an interview some-where.' She sighed. 'Do your best, girls.'

Fiona gave a resigned smile. After three months as a casualty doctor Damien Crewe was still sometimes more of a liability than an asset, although his lordly manner was inclined to suggest that the hospital might collapse without him.

Making for the ambulance entrance with Fiona, Shir-ley queried, 'What's wrong with Dr Crewe?'

'Oh, he'll be OK once he gets the corners knocked off,' Fiona returned charitably. 'He hasn't shaped up as quickly as some, that's all. Needs to be pointed in the right direction occasionally.'

She stopped by the doctor's office, interrupting his leisurely morning coffee. 'Damien, casualty on the way—a teenager, kicked in the face by her horse. She's in a bit of a state, they say.'

The young doctor raised a languid eyebrow and smoothed a hand over his straight blond hair. 'Someone should have warned her—never stand at the back end of a horse!' His eyes slid approvingly over Fiona's slender figure, her slim waist accentuated by the navy belt around the white dress. 'Do you ride?' he asked.

'Donkey rides on the sands when I was a kid, and that's my lot,' she said agreeably. 'You'll be along, will you?'

'Yah. . . I'll be there.' He returned to his coffee and the morning newspaper.

It was a skilful paramedic from the ambulance team who assisted the nurses to transfer the distraught teenager to the resuscitation-room, while Sister Bland took charge of the equally hysterical mother.

Crazed with pain and fear, the girl was holding a large dressing-pad over her mutilated face, crying and throwing herself about, out of control.

'Hello, Carly.' Fiona bent over the youngster, speaking in gentle tones. 'Will you let me see what the damage is?'

'Don't touch it! Don't touch it!' Carly squealed, getting the words out with difficulty and thrashing about, her long dark hair in a tangled spread.

'No, I won't touch it. Just let me look to see what's happened,' Fiona coaxed. She managed to lift the protective pad far enough to assess the quite serious damage to what had previously been a pretty face.

Her mother was wringing her hands, wailing, 'Oh, my God! She's lost—I don't know how many teeth. That wretched animal—he's ruined her looks. Do something for her—*please!*'

Sister Bland put a controlling hand on the woman's arm. 'The nurses will look after Carly. You come with me, dear, and give me a few details.'

In the examination-room Fiona talked to the youngster comfortingly. 'I know it must hurt a lot, sweetheart, but I'm sure there's nothing that can't be put right.

Let's get you out of this riding gear and into a gown to begin with.'

Shirley followed Fiona's lead of gentle persuasion and they managed to rid the girl of her jacket and tight jodhpurs to allow assessment of any further damage. Their soothing manner and expert handling had gone a long way to calming the terrified youngster while awaiting the arrival of the doctor.

Fiona was recording pulse and blood-pressure when Dr Crewe strolled in, stethoscope draped around his neck.

'So how are we getting on here?' he demanded, his voice at full volume. 'What's hiding under this, young lady?' His attempt to remove the bloodied dressing-pad resulted in violent resistance from the girl. She squirmed from side to side, making agonised squeaks of protest. 'Oh, come along now. This will get us nowhere,' Damien barked.

Fiona drew him to one side as Shirley sought to quieten the girl. 'Easy does it,' she murmured, 'the kid's petrified.'

Damien's idea of a subtle approach was to produce his pencil torch and attempt to examine the patient's pupils. 'Eyes open for me now, there's a good girl,' he boomed.

Her response was to screw her eyes more tightly shut and turn away whimpering when he tried to raise one of her eyelids.

'Little stinker!' he muttered, straightening up. He cast a despairing glance towards the nurses. 'Not going to co-operate, is she? Where the hell do I go from here? Get her X-rayed, I suppose, in case she's got a fractured mandible.'

Fiona shook her head. 'Out of the question for the

time being. I doubt she'd keep still long enough.' She paused thoughtfully. 'Why not give her a sedative and ward her until she's settled down at bit?'

She had barely finished speaking when Rory appeared on the scene, for which Fiona sent up a silent prayer of thanks. It seemed as though sanity came in with him, his very presence inspiring confidence.

'Is there a problem?' he asked quietly, having already been primed of the basic facts by Sister Bland.

'Er—well, sir, I could do with your opinion on this one.' Damien tossed back his flopping forelock.

Without waiting for further preamble Rory went to the bedside and took one of the youngster's hands between his own. Warily her eyes sought his and he smiled down at her.

'Hello, Carly. I'm Dr Kinross. There's nothing to be frightened of, you know. We want to help you.' His deep, melodious voice was reassuring yet authoritative. 'Now, I promise I won't touch your face, but I need to look. All right?' She allowed him to lift the dressing while he weighed up the damage. 'Can you open your mouth?' Tearfully she shook her head. He replaced the pad. 'Hmm. There's a fair bit of swelling. OK, Carly, we'll give you something for the pain. When you've had a little sleep you'll feel better, and then we'll let our facial experts see what they can do for you.'

Fiona prepared the injections he asked for.

'A tiny prick coming now,' he said. 'There you are, all done.' He patted her hand. 'I'll go and talk to your mother and then she can come and sit with you.'

The doctors left together, with Damien saying blandly, 'I was about to come to that course of action as you arrived, sir.'

'Ooh! Did you hear that?' Shirley murmured. 'What a creep! Kinross is terrific, though, isn't he?'

Fiona was lost in her own private world of admiration for this man with his tactical genius. She came back to realities and laughed. 'Yes, he can hold my hand any day if I'm sick.'

Later, having transferred the now docile Carly and her mother to the observation ward, Fiona was free to help out with the busy minor injuries clinic. As fate would have it, she again became involved in a disagreement with Damien.

The patient she was dealing with was a fleshy man with a fishhook embedded deeply in one of his fingers. Explaining the problem to the casualty officer, she said, 'It's impossible to push this through, Damien. It's a cut-down job, I'm afraid. I've put in a nerve block.'

'Well done!' He patted her condescendingly on the bottom and followed her to the treatment-room. 'Hello, sir. I suppose this was meant for the one that got away!' he exclaimed in jocular fashion. Scrubbing his hands elaborately before putting on rubber gloves, he sat down to inspect the swollen finger which Fiona had cushioned on a towel. He prodded it. 'Feel that?'

The patient acknowledged that his finger was numbed.

'Great! Scalpel, please, Nurse.' Damien held out his hand.

Fiona picked up a small piece of rubber flex from her dressing trolley. 'Tourniquet first?' she suggested.

'Good heavens, girl, we don't need that. My old boss would have sacked me on the spot,' he declared.

She gave him a warning glance. 'The barb's a long way in. You're likely to be flooded out.'

'I'll risk it. Let's get on,' he returned with some impatience.

As she had foreseen, the blood flowed freely once the incision was made and, although she swabbed constantly, location of the barb defeated him. Damien became more and more flustered. Finally, with a despairing glance towards Fiona, he said, 'See if Kinross can spare me a moment, will you?'

Hurrying along to the consultant's office, Fiona was relieved to find him still there. 'Sorry to trouble you,' she said, 'but Dr Crewe wonders if you can spare him a moment to look at a finger.'

'What's wrong with it?' asked Rory, getting up from his desk to follow her.

'It's a fishhook he's having trouble removing.'

In the treatment-room Rory took one look at the bloodied digit and murmured, 'That's something of a battleground!' He turned an enquiring glance to Fiona. 'Haven't you got a tourniquet there?'

'Yes,' she said, 'but——'

'Well, may I suggest it would be more use on the finger than on your trolley?' he cut in.

All her previous goodwill towards him vanished. *You pig!* she thought, gritting her teeth. She put on the tourniquet, shooting the silent Damien a withering glance while the consultant went to scrub up and take over.

Even with Rory's expertise, removal of the small elusive barb was a tricky business. 'That was no pushover,' he joked with the patient when the job was done. 'Nurse will put a bandage on it for you. Are you covered for tetanus?'

'Yes, I had a booster only recently,' the patient said.

'Good, but you'd better come back for an infection check in three days' time. All right?'

The doctors left, and Fiona bandaged the injury and covered it neatly with a tubular finger-stall.

'This is going to be sore for a day or two,' she sympathised.

'Yeah, I wish I'd had that last chap to begin with,' the man returned. 'He knew what he was doing.'

Fiona gave a wry smile. 'He should do—that was the consultant. See you in three days' time, then?'

Indulging in a few uncharitable thoughts about arrogant doctors, she cleaned up her trolley and then went off to lunch in the canteen.

Lois, her house-mate, was also on her lunch break, and they carried their food to an empty corner table, glad of the chance to chat. Talk soon got around to the forthcoming party.

'Who's taking Martin's place when he goes?' asked Fiona.

'Anna Fuller. Don't you know her?' Lois asked. 'She's been with us a month already. Lives in one of those flats across the road from us.'

'Oh, that redhead.' Fiona had a mental image of the striking girl in her trim navy uniform.

'Yes, she comes from Glasgow. I like her. She and Kinross are quite matey. Well, that's only natural, I suppose, both being from Scotland,' Lois reflected.

'Mmm, I suppose so.' Fiona concentrated on her Welsh rarebit for a moment. 'Will Rory be at the party, do you think?'

'More than likely, since he's all in favour of staff socialising.' Lois gave a sideways grin. 'Why? Are you interested?'

'Huh! I'm rapidly going right off him, sarcastic swine!'

Fiona relieved her feelings by telling about the incident of the fishhook. 'And it was Damien who decided against using a tourniquet. He's the doctor. What was I supposed to do?'

Lois simply giggled. 'Life's full of injustices, doll. Never mind. Come shopping tonight? I need some new gear for the party.'

'OK. And I've got to get something special for my brother's engagement party.' Fiona brightened. 'Meet you in reception at four-thirty.'

They parted company and, returning to A and E, Fiona paused to study the staff notice-board. Among the many items was one which had newly appeared, inviting applications for the vacancy created by Sister Bland's forthcoming departure.

'Too late to change your mind now, Molly,' she joked, reporting back. 'Your job's being advertised on the notice-board.'

'I know, and it'll be in the nursing Press next week, so get your application in, Fiona.'

'I don't think Kinross would consider me a suitable candidate,' Fiona returned with a short laugh.

'Rubbish!' Molly declared. 'Time you took the plunge, and you'll never be more ready than you are now. Pop along to Personnel and get yourself an application form.'

It was a moderately quiet afternoon for a Saturday, punctuated by the usual sprains and cuts. Fiona's most interesting patient was a young man stung on the neck by a wasp at the bakery where he worked. Rushed in by his alarmed boss, he had a dangerously strong reaction, with swelling of throat, tongue and lips.

Although the only doctor on hand was once again Damien, this time he was equal to the occasion, recognising the need for urgent treatment with anti-histamines.

'Hydrocortisone and piriton—stat., Fiona,' he drawled importantly.

The dosage checked and injections given, she kept a close watch on the patient for a couple of hours. His reactions subsiding, he was then able to be discharged on a short course of the drugs.

Fiona had been aware that Rory was once again in the department, having been called to deal with a rugby-playing casualty. She'd been hoping for a chance to speak to him, and now, as he was about to leave at the same time as herself, the opportunity came.

'Off home?' he asked pleasantly, strolling along with her towards the reception area where she'd agreed to meet Lois.

'No, I'm going shopping,' she said.

His blue eyes sparkled wickedly. 'To cheer yourself up after a day of coping with Dr Crewe?'

'No, I can handle Damien. It's the doctors who jump to conclusions whom I find impossible,' she returned.

He half smiled. 'Is that remark directed at me?' When she didn't answer, he went on, 'I don't go about with my eyes shut, you know.'

She was silent for a moment, feeling a little awkward about what she wanted to say, although there was no reason why she should. 'Rory. . .' She hesitated. 'About James's party, I need to take my own car up to Hampstead that weekend, so I won't be travelling with you. Thanks all the same.'

'Oh, why's that?' he asked.

'Well, as I told you, my friend Craig is coming back from Florida. I'll be meeting him at Heathrow that

Friday morning. His plane gets in at eight-thirty, so I'm going up the night before, or I'd never make it.'

His steady, appraising gaze ruffled her careful composure. 'Ah! The absentee boyfriend,' he said. 'Will this be the big showdown?'

She let out a long breath. 'I don't know, do I? It might be. Or I might fall madly in love with him when I see him again,' she added facetiously.

'Hmm. So I suppose I shall just have to look forward to seeing you at the party?'

'Yes, no way would I miss that. And I've got four days, so I shan't be travelling back till the Monday. You'll be leaving on Sunday, will you?'

'Probably. But that's still a fortnight away. Are you a busy girl until then?'

'Desperately,' she joked, and, catching sight of Lois hovering nearby, 'Must go, Rory—I'm wasting good shopping time. Goodnight.'

Flashing him a bright smile, she hurried to join her friend. 'Sorry about that, Lo. He was feeling chatty.'

Lois gave her a droll look. 'For someone who's rapidly going off someone. . . I didn't detect any bad vibes.'

'I'm a good actress,' Fiona grinned. 'Shall we take my car? Then I'll bring you back here to pick up yours.'

They drove to a shopping mall on the outskirts of town since it had extended shopping hours.

In a fashionable boutique Fiona tried on a number of dresses and eventually fell for a sparkly black cocktail dress with a wide neckline and sleek wrapover skirt. She twirled for her friend's approval.

'That's gorgeous,' Lois enthused. 'Really trendy. Makes me wish Martin's do was going to be a dress-up affair instead of the usual casual do.'

Lois bought black leggings and a stylish green overshirt for the occasion, complementing the outfit with some chunky gold earrings. Fiona decided to make do with casual gear she already had, having spent more on the dress then she intended.

Both pleased with their purchases, after dropping in to a cafeteria for a light snack they set off back to the hospital to collect Lois's car. With her eyes on the road, Fiona didn't spot the driver of the red car who sped past them in the opposite direction, but Lois turned her head to get a better look.

'That was Kinross,' she said, 'and Sister Fuller with him. Looks as if they're even matier than I thought.'

Fiona smiled but said nothing. After setting Lois and her packages down by her car, she drove on home, her thoughts beset by the consultant. Why should she care if Rory was bestowing his favours on someone else? He was an attractive man; it had been bound to happen sooner or later. There was no reason for her to feel aggrieved—that was being ridiculous. All the same, she couldn't help feeling dispirited.

On the night of Martin's farewell party Fiona and Lois decided to take a taxi to Mallard's Island, thinking parking might be a problem. It was a mild and mellow evening as they crossed the footbridge to the floating hostelry, the public bars of which were already busy with their usual customers.

Upstairs in the room let for private gatherings the strobe lights flashed; the DJ had already got the music going, while Martin welcomed all his guests with his usual *bonhomie*. And Sister Anna Fuller was standing with him. In a pair of soft green culottes and toning floral blouse, her bright hair pinned up in a topknot, she presented a pleasing picture.

'Hi, girls!' Martin greeted both Lois and Fiona with a kiss. 'Great to see you—even if it is a sad occasion for me. Fiona, do you know Anna, my replacement? Fiona's one of the best pairs of hands in Casualty,' he said in a stage whisper to Anna, 'although don't let on I said so.'

Fiona grinned. 'Don't overdo it, now. Hello, Anna,' she said. 'Hope you'll like it here.'

The redhead smiled broadly. 'I'm sure I shall. Sweet of Martin to let me share his party, isn't it? I wasn't going to butt in, but he insisted.'

Martin waved a bountiful hand. 'Go and find a drink, girls, and let your hair down, eh?'

More people were arriving, corks were popping, the DJ was full of merry quips and camaraderie prevailed. Over by the bar Fiona helped herself to white wine and then sought out Adrian, whom she found standing alone looking a little glum. 'Cheer up,' she said gaily, 'it may never happen!'

He laughed. 'Do I look that bad? Actually I was thinking about an interview I had, wondering if I'd blown it.'

'What were you applying for?' she asked.

'Surgical registrar—I'd like to specialise in transplant surgery eventually.'

'Anyone who turns you down needs a brain transplant,' Fiona declared. 'Think positive.' She put down her glass, her feet itching to dance. 'Come and have a bop and forget your worries.'

'I'm not the world's greatest mover,' he warned, finishing his own drink.

She took his hand and pulled him on to the dance-floor, swivelling her jeans-clad hips invitingly to the music. Blonde hair framing her captivating face, her sparkle was infectious. 'That doesn't matter,' she said, 'just do your own thing.'

There was no doubt about it, Adrian had little sense of rhythm, but he tried, and after a hilarious session he departed cheerfully to get them both a long drink.

The dancing had also helped to relieve some of Fiona's tension which had been building while her eyes searched the crowd for a glimpse of Rory. Now, suddenly, she saw him. Tall and striking and every inch the professional in his well-tailored suit, he was in easy conversation with Martin and the attractive Anna.

Fiona's heart bounded alarmingly. She averted her gaze as his eyes strayed in her direction, as if feeling her attention. Adrian arrived back with the drinks.

'Oh, thanks! You're a life-saver. It's getting so warm in here.' She fanned her pink cheeks with her hand.

'Kinross looks in good form,' Adrian remarked. 'I want to have a word with him about my reference.'

'No worries there, I should think. You're the best cas man I've worked with in a long time,' she encouraged.

He gave a modest smile. 'Nice of you to say so.'

There followed a break in the music and the presentation of gifts to Martin, after which Rory stepped forward to give his own personal tribute to the charge nurse.

'Although I haven't known Martin for as long as some of you,' the consultant said, 'it's been quite long enough to know that I regret having to lose him. His successor will have a hard act to follow,' he went on with a sideways smile at Anna Fuller. After a few more well-chosen remarks, Rory charged everyone to raise their glasses and drink to Martin's success.

The formalities over, dancing continued, and Fiona found herself confronted by Damien.

'Will you do me the honour?' he said, inviting her on to the floor with an exaggerated bow.

She widened her eyes, but went along with him all the same. 'I should be giving you the brush-off after the way you dropped me in it the other day,' she reminded him. 'I'm too forgiving, that's my trouble.'

'We do have to keep our handmaidens toeing the line, you know,' he smirked.

'Watch it! That kind of talk will get you a knee where it hurts.'

Damien laughed. 'You wouldn't dare. Anyway, that my sweet, would be completely out of character. Whoops!' Their progress came to a halt as he backed into Rory, who was standing on the perimeter, watching. 'Oh, sorry, sir. I'm finding this girl something of a handful. . .'

'Then I shall relieve you of the responsibility,' Rory said, and calmly took possession of Fiona himself. He looked down at her with a questioning smile. 'You didn't mind, I hope?'

A tremor passed over her at the touch of his hands. 'Not in the least. He's not my top of the pops at the moment,' she confessed. 'I can't think why he asked me.'

The consultant looked amused. 'Doesn't everyone want to dance with the prettiest girl in the room?'

She sighed tolerantly. 'I thought we'd agreed, you don't need to ply me with the social chat, Rory. We're almost like family. We can be honest with each other, remember?'

He chuckled. 'Yes, I remember. And I *never* go in for false flattery. Remember that.'

She wrinkled her nose at him, and he gathered her closer, and they moved around the crowded hall, their bodies perfectly attuned. 'This reminds me of my student days,' he murmured presently, between crooning bits of the old romantic melody being played.

Fiona wondered if it also reminded him of happier times, before the tragedy in his life. Not that he seemed sad. In fact, she sensed he was enjoying their closeness as much as she was.

Yet her own pleasure was tinged with melancholy. If it had not been for family connections, would Rory even have noticed her? she wondered. But whatever it was that motivated him, there was no reason why she shouldn't enjoy the friendship he offered. Just so long as he didn't discover that she was half in love with him and getting more so by the minute.

All around them couples were flirting and affairs were beginning to blossom. With her senses seduced by Rory's nearness, Fiona found herself caught up in the potent atmosphere. An intensity of longing surged through her. Impulsively her arms slid around his neck and she rested her head against his broad chest.

'Effie?' He put a hand under her chin and tilted her dreamy-eyed face to his. 'How much have you had to drink?' he asked with a puzzled smile.

The spell was broken. She was piqued that he had called her back from fantasyland. 'Hardly anything,' she retorted. 'Why?'

'I just wondered. Will you be driving yourself home?'

'No. Lois and I came by taxi.'

'Well, don't bother to get one back. I'll take you.'

The music had faded out and the magic had gone. She glared up into his authoritative face. 'For goodness' sake! There's no need to play Big Brother. I'll make my own arrangements, thank you. Besides, there's Lois to consider.'

'She can come with us, although I think she might

very well be otherwise engaged.' Rory glanced to where Lois and Martin stood locked in each other's arms.

Fiona looked, and shrugged. 'I did wonder if they might be heading that way. Well, excuse me, Rory,' she went on, being determinedly bright, 'this is my cheer-up-Adrian night.' And she went back to where she had left the young casualty doctor.

Adrian said, 'You never did tell me how you came to know Rory so well.'

'Not a lot to tell. Only that he and my brother were college mates. Now he seems to have appointed himself my watchdog. Sickening, isn't it?'

'Lucky you!' Adrian chuckled. 'Can't be bad, having someone of his calibre on your side.'

'I don't know that he is,' she said. Although she made a great effort to enter into the spirit of things, the heart had gone out of it for Fiona. She couldn't help it that her eyes were constantly following Rory. He was now danc-ing with Anna. The new sister would be in her late twenties, Fiona judged, which was nearer his age-group than her own. She wished she had a few more years under her belt.

Adrian's attention was also on the newcomer. 'She's stunning, isn't she?' he said.

'Why don't you ask her to dance?' Fiona prompted.

He sighed. 'You saw how I perform. Wish I could dance. It's a great social asset.'

'Well, go and talk to her, anyway. I'm sure she'd be pleased.'

Damien came to claim another dance with her, and when next she saw Adrian Anna was laughingly guiding him around the floor.

'Kinross had a nerve, pinching my girl, the cheeky devil,' Damien said, whirling her expertly in a quickstep.

'I'm not your girl,' Fiona said, smiling.

'You could be, if you play your cards right.'

'I don't play cards either,' she returned.

Damien raised a provocative eyebrow. 'You don't ride? You don't play cards? It's high time someone took you in hand, my sweet. We'll talk about it in my car on the way home, hmm?'

She shook her head. 'Thanks all the same, but I've made arrangements for getting home.'

'Silly girl. Can't you unmake them?' He brushed her nose with his.

'Sorry, Damien, I couldn't.' On the pretext of needing to talk to Lois, she escaped his company.

The evening came to an end with the customary circle for 'Auld Lang Syne', and, making their way to the cloakroom afterwards, Lois confided,

'Martin's taking me home, Fiona, but you can come with us. That's OK.'

'Oh, don't worry about me,' Fiona returned. 'Rory has offered.' She laughed. 'He said he'd take us both too, but I'll tell him you're fixed up.'

After she had collected her jacket, she found the consultant standing near the exit as though waiting for her appearance.

'It's got to be you after all,' she told him gaily. 'I thought I'd be safer with you than with Damien.'

'You did, did you?' A smile escaped the corners of his mouth. They joined the throng going down the stairs and over the footbridge. 'Does that mean you trust me— or that you think I'm past it?'

She watched the tavern's fairy lights dancing in the dark water, wondering if he had any idea of the disturbing effect he had on her. 'Yes. And no,' she said.

He considered that for a moment, taking her hand to

guide her in the direction of his car. 'Yes and no? Almost a contradiction in terms, isn't it?'

They reached his car without further comment, but once seated and on their way, he remarked, 'Was it my imagination, or did you go out of your way to avoid me tonight?'

'Of course not. I just felt Adrian needed some moral support, that's all. At first he was sort of despondent, about the results of an interview he had.'

'Well, your efforts appear to have paid off,' Rory said. 'When I saw Adrian he was well away with Sister Fuller and looking cheerful. And speaking of sisters, have you applied for Sister Bland's post yet?'

'I've picked up an application form, but I haven't had time to fill it in so far.'

'It's not going to fill itself in,' he pointed out, quietly critical. 'You should get a move on, or you'll miss the boat.'

'I will, I will. Don't harass me.'

He grinned. 'Somebody should. As I told you, opportunities have to be seized.'

'Oh, dry up,' she said.

Much to her relief they had arrived at Sycamore Grange. Rory braked, switched off the engine and turned towards her. 'What would you say if I said that *I* was in need of some moral support?' he asked, a glint of mischief in his eyes.

'You? *You* need about as much moral support as— as—the Archangel Gabriel,' she scoffed.

He passed a despairing hand over his face. 'Oh, God! I don't know how I acquired that kind of reputation.'

'Want to come in for coffee?' she asked.

For a long moment he studied her without speaking. What was going on behind those dark-fringed eyes she had no idea, but there was a kind of alchemy at work which fired her senses. All at once he leaned towards her and planted a firm kiss on her lips. 'Perhaps you'd better go,' he said, 'before the Archangel Gabriel becomes the fallen angel Lucifer.'

Her body taut with longing, Fiona opened the car door and urged her reluctant limbs to walk towards the house.

'Goodnight!' he called, starting up his engine as she put her key in the door.

Casually she turned to wave, managing to hold back the tears until he drove away.

Why, oh, why did he have to come back to this particular spot on the globe? Fiona agonised. She'd been completely happy here until he put in an appearance.

# CHAPTER SIX

THE last of the Indian summer had rolled away in a splendour of autumn tints, followed by soggy leaves underfoot, coughs and colds and the usual ailments that accompanied the approach of winter. Already Christmas cards were on sale in the shops, along with other seasonal reminders. But for Fiona there were other things to occupy her before giving a thought to Christmas.

She had written to Craig saying she was looking forward to meeting him at Heathrow, and she had handed in her application for the sister's job. Her c.v. had read quite impressively when she had listed all her school and nursing qualifications.

It was the Thursday before Fiona's eventful weekend that Aileen asked her casually, during their coffee break, whether she'd heard anything about who had got the job.

'No, I haven't heard a thing,' Fiona said. 'Have you?'

Aileen scowled. 'I just got a letter through the post this morning saying I hadn't been successful.'

'Oh! Well, my rejection's probably on its way, then,' Fiona returned, not unduly worried.

She was somewhat surprised when Molly Bland came to find her later that day, as she was strapping a sprained ankle, and said, 'When you've finished here, Fiona, the SNO would like to see you in her office. Er—don't get too excited, though,' she added, her round face non-committal.

After completing her task with a pleasant word to the

patient, Fiona hurried along to the staff-room to tidy her hair and readjust her blue-bordered cap before making for the senior nursing officer's quarters. She could only assume it had something to do with her application, and it was with a degree of panic that she knocked at the door. On being invited to enter she was surprised to find Mrs Newsome alone. Fiona had expected to find two of the consultants there as well, if she were being interviewed.

'Nurse Rogers—sit down, my dear.' The SNO waved her to a chair and reached for a folder full of papers, adjusting her glasses as she leafed through them until she found the one that she wanted.

Hands clasped in her lap, Fiona waited, recognising her own application form for the sister's post.

'Your qualifications do you credit,' Mrs Newsome said, removing her spectacles as she looked up. 'I'm very sorry, but I'm afraid on this occasion we have to disappoint you.'

'Oh, I see,' Fiona murmured, not knowing quite how she felt.

'In normal circumstances you would have been an ideal candidate for Sister Bland's position,' the nursing officer went on. 'However, the fact is that Sister North— at present full-time on nights—wishes to come back on to days, and we felt it only right to accommodate her. But we shall certainly keep you in mind for the future,' she said. 'Your references are excellent.'

Fiona rose to leave. 'Well, thanks for taking the trouble to tell me yourself, Mrs Newsome.'

The other woman smiled. 'We didn't want you to be discouraged. You're young, Fiona. Your chance will come.'

Going back to her work, Fiona was relieved that the

matter was finally settled. Now she could just enjoy doing her job and Rory would have no cause to chivvy her.

'You knew, didn't you?' she said, reporting back to Molly.

The sister pulled rueful face. 'Yes, and I'm sorry. Apparently Sally North's domestic circumstances have changed, and since she's already a sister and with good A and E experience, that was it.'

'Really, I don't mind,' Fiona confessed. 'My life is a bit complicated just now. I'd rather just jog along as I am for the time being.'

Molly breathed a sigh of relief. 'Thank goodness you didn't react like Aileen! Anyone would think it was my personal fault she didn't get the job.'

'Maybe it's as well I didn't get it, then,' Fiona chuckled.

'Back to the present, then,' Molly said. 'We're expecting a psychopath from the local lock-up. He's a self-mutilator—slashed his own arm extensively. He'll need tactful handling. Thank goodness we've got Kinross we can call on. I dread to think how Damien. . .' She broke off as three burly prison officers hove into view along with the casualty.

'Where do you want him, Sister?' one of them asked.

'Nurse will show you. I'll get a doctor to come along and see him.'

Molly bustled away, leaving Fiona to show the party to the treatment room.

The patient was a young man of about Fiona's own age. Slight of build, everything about him was in faded sepia tones—sallow skin, pale brown eyes, lank brown hair and a defeated expression. Although there was blood everywhere over his hands and his clothing, there seemed no obvious arterial bleeding.

'Hello!' Fiona said kindly, addressing her remarks to the prisoner and not his keepers. 'What's your name?'

'Mickey Mouse,' he muttered.

She curbed a smile. 'Well, come and sit down and let's see what we can do for you.'

The three warders kept a vigilant guard as she removed his prison-issue denim jacket and blue-striped cotton shirt. Carefully she cut away the makeshift blood-soaked bandages that swathed his injured arm. There were a number of long, ugly slashes, some fairly deep.

'What did you do this with?' she queried.

'Ask no questions, hear no lies,' he snarled.

'Watch it, lad,' one of the warders put in. 'It's for your benefit she wants to know. A kitchen knife it was, Nurse,' he told Fiona.

Sister Bland returned accompanied by the consultant, who examined the patient with his usual courtesy. 'Well, there seems to be no nerve damage, fortunately,' he pronounced after making tests, 'and there's no deep vessel involvement. Straightforward suturing for the large wounds, Nurse. Steri-strips for these minor cuts.'

Motioning Fiona to follow him outside, Rory murmured, 'It's going to be a long job, and you'll have to be diplomatic. Can you handle it?'

'Yes, I'll be fine,' she assured him.

'I'll send Rosemary along to help. Any sign of trouble, let us know at once,' Molly said.

Back in the treatment-room Fiona uncovered her dressings trolley and set out her equipment. 'Will you get up on the bed, please?' she directed smoothly. 'You'll be more comfortable there. I'm going to put in some local anaesthetic before I start cleaning you up. That'll sting a little at first, but once it takes effect you'll be OK.'

Drawing up lignocaine into a hypodermic, she expertly injected small amounts on either side of the large wounds, apologising as he winced. 'Sorry about this, but it's nearly done, Mickey.' She smiled at him. 'Your name's not really Mickey, is it?'

His tension seemed to ease. 'No, it's Stuart. What's yours, mate?'

'Fiona,' she told him civilly, refilling her hypodermic syringe and carrying on injecting. That task finished, she poured Savlon solution into a gallipot and, when the anaesthetic had taken effect, she cleansed the wounds before suturing.

Rosemary had arrived to help with opening up sterile packs, and presently, scrubbed up and gloved, Fiona was able to start the long, tedious business of repair. The prison officers, meanwhile, gossiped among themselves while keeping an eagle eye on their prisoner. Fiona endeavoured to humour her patient with harmless small talk as stitch after stitch was tied off.

Standing by, Rosemary grew increasingly pale. Suddenly she put a hand to her mouth, mumbled 'Sorry!' and rushed from the room.

'What's the matter with 'er?' the patient demanded. 'She scared of me or something?'

'No, probably feeling queasy. She's just a student,' Fiona explained. 'It takes time to get used to emergency work.'

The prisoner grew less taciturn. 'How long you been doing this sort of thing?' he wanted to know.

His haunted eyes gave her the shivers. She concentrated on the job in hand while answering, 'I've been nursing for six years—doing this job for about two.'

In the face of her friendly manner his hostility subsided. When, some fifty sutures later, she had at last finished and anchored his injured arm in a high sling, he held out his other hand to shake hers.

'Thanks, Fiona. You're ace,' he said.

'My pleasure.' She gave him a sympathetic smile and wished him good luck.

The prison officers took their charge away, and Fiona stretched her aching shoulders and sighed, wondering what had landed the man in prison.

Rosemary reappeared with a penitent expression on her pale face. 'Terribly sorry to let you down, Fiona. I came over all peculiar—thought I was going to throw up. I hope you didn't need me any more.'

'No, I managed. Not to worry—it happens,' Fiona reassured the youngster. 'You'll get used to it. If you're feeling better now, though, you can help me with the clearing up. It's nearly time I was gone.'

'Yes, of course.' Rosemary stripped off the used disposable covering on the bed and replaced it with a fresh one. 'He was an odd-looking bloke, wasn't he? Gave me the creeps. Fancy cutting himself about like that! Why was he in the nick—what had he done?'

Fiona shrugged. 'I don't know. Best not to ask questions—it's not our business. He was brought for treatment, and that's what he got.' She spread a fresh cloth over the dressings trolley which she had cleaned and re-set. 'There, that's my lot. Now I've got four lovely days off. 'Bye, Ros.'

By now it was past four-thirty, and as Fiona scooted along to the staff-room to change, Rory—about to leave the department—stopped her in her tracks. 'I did look in to check you were all right,' he said, 'and you were.

So you think you've earned your long weekend?' He gave her one of his mind-blowing smiles.

'I jolly well have!' She swallowed against the customary flutter in her throat, finding his steady gaze more disconcerting than a dozen difficult patients.

'And how are you feeling about this meeting with the boyfriend?' he enquired mildly.

'A bit apprehensive. But Craig is a reasonable sort of guy.'

Rory laughed. 'So are most normal people, most of the time. But being crossed in love can cause fireworks. That was your last patient's problem.'

'Was it?' She looked into his teasing eyes. 'Oh, stop trying to scare me. Craig's not likely to go berserk. He's a phlegmatic Englishman.'

'He must be very phlegmatic to leave his girl for a year and expect her to be waiting when he gets back.' His dark brows lifted a fraction. 'Do you think he's been faithful?'

'How should I know? I rather hope not. It would make me feel less guilty about calling it a day.' She fidgeted impatiently and checked the time on her pendant watch. 'Anyway, must dash. See you on Saturday.'

'Yes, I'm looking forward to it.'

Fiona's journey was trouble-free, and by eight o'clock that evening she was driving across the dusky greenness of Hampstead Heath towards her brother's home in a tree-lined road of attractive villas.

An affectionate welcome from both James and Deborah greeted her arrival. Her brother—almost as tall as Rory—caught her up in his arms and gave her a resounding kiss. 'Great to see you, Eff.'

Deborah, waiting her turn to greet their visitor, smiled

tolerantly. She was a tall slim girl and looked as elegant as ever in black ski-pants and a cherry-red sweater, her sleek dark hair cut in a geometric style. 'James, find us all a drink, darling,' she said, after her own exchange of a hug and kiss. 'Dinner's nearly ready.'

'Where's the ring, then, Debs?' Fiona demanded as they all made towards the large kitchen.

The emerald and diamond cluster duly displayed, she sighed, 'Oh, that's really gorgeous! Have you fixed a date for the wedding?'

'Ten days before Christmas, so make sure you arrange your off-duty. And I'd like you to be my bridesmaid,' Deborah said.

'I'd love to!' Fiona sipped the Martini her brother handed her.

'Great. Then we can talk clothes before you go back.' Deborah returned.

'And will there be a ring on your finger when you see Craig again?' James asked his sister.

She shook her head. 'Pretty definitely *no*, unless I have an amazing change of heart. A year's a long time, and feelings alter.'

'What about absence making the heart grow fonder?' Deborah ventured.

'Perhaps she's met someone else?' James eyed his sister enquiringly. 'I shall have to ask Rory what you've been getting up to.'

'Don't you dare!' Fiona protested. 'Just because we happen to work at the same place it doesn't mean he knows what goes on in my life.'

'Hmm!' her brother pondered. 'He probably knows more about you than you realise.'

She made a face at him and changed the subject. 'I'm

# ★★★★★★ PLAY ★★★★★★
# £600,000 LOTTO!

★★★★★★★★★★★★★★★★★★★★★★★

## NO COST... NO OBLIGATION...

## NO PURCHASE NECESSARY!

IT'S FUN

IT'S FREE

**FREE BOOKS!**
**CASH PRIZES!**

# LOTTO PRIZE DRAW
# RULES AND REGULATIONS

**NO PURCHASE OR OBLIGATION NECESSARY TO ENTER THE PRIZE DRAW**

**1** To enter the Prize Draw and join our Reader Service, follow the directions published. The method of entry may vary. For eligibility, Prize Draw entries must be received no later than 31st March 1994. No liability is assumed for printing errors, lost, late or misdirected entries and unreadable entries. Mechanically reproduced entries are null and void.

**2** Whether you join our Reader Service or not your prize draw numbers will be compared against a list of randomly, pre-selected prize winning numbers to determine prize winners. In the event that all prizes are not claimed via the return of prize winning numbers, random draws will be held from among all other entries received to award unclaimed prizes. These prizes are in addition to any free gifts that may be offered.

**3** Prize winners will be determined no later than 30th May 1994. Selection of the winning numbers and random draws are under the supervision of D. L. Blair Inc., an independent judging organization whose decisions are final. One prize only to a family or organisation. No substitution will be made for any prize, except as offered. Taxes and duties on all prizes are the sole responsibility of winners. Winners will be notified by mail. The chances of winning are determined by the number of entries distributed and received.

**4** This Prize Draw is open to residents of the United Kingdom, U.S.A., Canada, France, Germany and Eire; 18 years of age or older except employees and their immediate family members of Torstar Corporation, D. L. Blair Inc., their affiliates, subsidiaries, and all other agencies, entities, and persons connected with the use, marketing or conduct of this Prize Draw. All applicable laws and regulations apply.

**5** Winners of major prizes will be obligated to sign and return an affidavit of eligibility and release of liability within 30 days of notification. In the event of non-compliance within this time period, prizes may be awarded to alternative winners. Any prize or prize notification returned as undeliverable, will result in the awarding of that prize to an alternative winner. By acceptance of their prize, winners consent to the use of their names, photographs or other likenesses for the purposes of advertising, trade and promotion on behalf of Torstar Corporation, without further compensation, unless prohibited by law.

**6** This Prize Draw is presented by Torstar Corporation, its subsidiaries, and affiliates in conjunction with book, merchandise and/or product offerings. Prizes are as follows:-

**Grand Prize** - £600.000 (payable at £20,000 a year for 30 years).

The First through to the Sixth Prizes may be presented in different creative executions, each with the following approximate values:

| | | |
|---|---|---|
| **First Prize** | | - £25,000 |
| **Second Prize** | | - £ 6,000 |
| **Third Prize** | (x 2) | - £ 3,000 each |
| **Fourth Prize** | (x 5) | - £ 600 each |
| **Fifth Prize** | (x 10) | - £ 150 each |
| **Sixth Prize** | (x 1,000) | - £ 60 each |

**7** Prize winners will have the opportunity of selecting any alternative prize offered for that level. Torstar Corporation may present this Prize Draw utilizing names other than 'Million Dollar Sweepstakes'.

For a current list of prize options offered and all names that Prize Draws may utilise, send a stamped self-addressed envelope marked 'Prize Draw 94 Options' to the address below.

**For a list of prize winners** (available after 31st July 1994) send a stamped self-addressed envelope marked 'Prize Draw 94 Winners' to the address below.

**Prize Draw address:**
Mills & Boon Reader Service,
PO Box 236, Croydon, CR9 3RU.

# Mills & Boon invite you to play
# £600,000 LOTTO!

**LOTTO CARD No:  SA**   537995

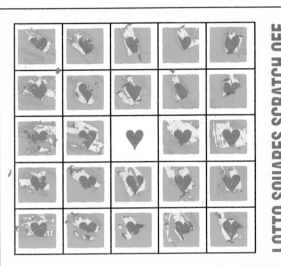

**LOTTO SQUARES SCRATCH OFF**

**Instructions:** Using a coin edge, scratch away 4 or 5 silver squares in a straight line (across, down or diagonally). If 5 hearts are revealed, this card is eligible to win the £600,000 Grand Prize: If 4 hearts, £25,000; 3 hearts, £6,000; 2 hearts, £3,000; 1 heart, £600. VOID IF MORE THAN 5 SILVER SQUARES ARE SCRATCHED AWAY.

## AND...
## YOU CAN CLAIM A MILLS & BOON ROMANCE ABSOLUTELY FREE AND WITH NO OBLIGATION

To register your entry in the draw and to claim your free book simply return this card. Don't forget to send us your address!

## DON'T HESITATE - REPLY TODAY!

# LOTTO REGISTRATION CARD

**YES,** please register my entry in the £600,000 Lotto Prize novel. I understand that I am under no obligation whatsoever.

Draw. And, please send me my FREE Romantic

3A3PD

Ms / Mrs / Miss / Mr _____

Address _____

_____

_____ Postcode _____

Signature _____

Please note that the offer expires on 30th September 1993 and is subject to availability. Only one application per household. Readers overseas please send for postage details. In Southern Africa write to Book Services International Ltd., P.O. Box 24654, Craighall, transvaal 2024. You will receive further information from Mills & Boon about how you can receive more FREE books and gifts.

You may be mailed with offers from other reputable companies as a result of this application. If you would rather not take advantage of these opportunities, please tick this box ☐

MILLS & BOON
READER SERVICE
**FREEPOST**
P.O. BOX 236
CROYDON
SURREY
CR9 9EL

NO
STAMP
NEEDED

# ARE YOU A FAN
# OF MILLS & BOON
# MEDICAL ROMANCES?

IF YOU are a regular United Kingdom buyer of Mills &
Boon Medical Romances you might like to tell us your
opinion of the books we publish to help us in publishing
the books *you* like.

Mills & Boon have a Reader Panel of Medical Romance
readers. Each person on the panel receives a
questionnaire every third month asking her for *her*
opinion of the past twelve Medical Romances. All people
who send in their replies have a chance of winning a
FREE year's supply of Medical Romances.

If YOU would like to be considered for inclusion on the
Panel please give us details about yourself below. We
can't guarantee that everyone will be on the panel but
first come will be first considered. All postage will be free.
Younger readers are particularly welcome.

Year of birth ................. Month ................

Age at completion of full-time education ...............

Single ☐ Married ☐ Widowed ☐ Divorced ☐

If any children at home, their ages please .............

Your name (print please) ........................

Address ...................................

.........................................

.................... Postcode ................

## THANK YOU! PLEASE TEAR OUT AND POST
## NO STAMP NEEDED IN THE U.K.

DR/0393/RD

# 2

BUSINESS REPLY SERVICE
Licence No. SF195

MILLS & BOON READER PANEL
P.O. BOX 152,
SHEFFIELD S11 8TE

Postage
will be
paid by
Mills & Boon
Limited

jolly glad you two finally decided to get your act together.'

James put his arm around Deborah's shoulders and kissed the back of her neck as she inspected the contents of a saucepan. 'I decided she was too good a cook to let slip through my fingers,' he said, whereupon she flicked him around the head with her tea-towel.

'Men!' she declared, rolling her eyes.

After the evening meal they sat and talked endlessly, catching up with family news. At last Deborah yawned and said she simply must go to bed. 'I'm on an early tomorrow,' she remembered.

'Oh, and I've got to be up early as well,' Fiona said. 'Got to be at Heathrow by eight-thirty.'

Working it out, her brother decided she should allow at least an hour. 'It'll take him time to get through Customs, but the morning traffic will be heavy on the motorway.'

'Do bring Craig back here if you want to,' Deborah suggested. 'There'll be nobody in until five o'clock, so I'll give you a key.'

James put in, 'And he's welcome at our party, of course, unless he's got other plans for Saturday.'

Rain was pattering on the bedroom window when Fiona awoke the following morning. It was dark outside and she was loath to get up. Most of all she didn't relish the thought of the meeting awaiting her. Life, she reflected, was full of having to face up to things you would rather avoid. Reluctantly throwing off the duvet, she washed at the fitted washbasin in her room, pulled on jeans and a primrose polo-necked sweater and skipped downstairs for a quick coffee with Deborah. Then, after checking that the flight was due in on time, she picked up her denim jacket and set out to drive to the airport.

As James had predicted, the roads were congested and the traffic often at a frustrating crawl, and it was really not Fiona's fault that the plane had landed and disgorged its passengers before she arrived. Being no stranger to Heathrow, she wasted no time in finding her way to the car park and thence to the upper level overlooking the arrival lounge, from where she scanned the crowds.

Craig was easy to spot—the tall fellow with the healthy tan, his straight brown hair a little longer than when she had last seen him. Wearing a brown suede jacket over black jeans and a cream sweater, he was standing with his luggage trolley and glancing impatiently around the thronging concourse where other passengers were already reunited with friends and relatives.

Fiona sped to meet him, her fair hair flying, her cheeks pink. 'Craig! Oh, I'm so sorry I'm late,' she panted. 'Have you been here long?'

He grinned a welcome and they kissed. 'It's a woman's prerogative, I suppose, being late.'

'I couldn't help it, honestly. The traffic was frightful!' They stood looking at each other a little awkwardly, almost like strangers, and she felt oddly shy. 'It's been a long time,' she said.

'Yes, a whole year since you refused to follow my good example,' he chided, smiling.

She ignored the rebuke. 'Well, you're back again now. What shall we. . . I mean, where would you like me to take you?'

'Shall we have some coffee first? I'd rather like to talk before we go anywhere.'

'OK,' she agreed lightly, but her stomach knotted at his earnest tone of voice.

They wandered in the direction of a coffee bar. Finding an unoccupied but cluttered table, Fiona cleared it and stayed with his luggage while he went to buy the drinks. Then, sitting opposite each other, they exchanged self-conscious smiles.

'You're prettier then ever.' Craig suddenly leaned forward and stroked her cheek. He sighed heavily. 'All the way over I've been wondering how to put this, and seeing you doesn't make it any easier.'

She gave a small shrug of encouragement. 'Just say what's on your mind. That's best isn't it?'

'I suppose so.' He tore open a sachet of brown sugar, tipped it into his coffee and stirred before going on. 'The truth is, Fiona, I'm not home for good. I've extended my contract for another year at least. I'm going back again directly after Christmas.'

Fiona's mouth gaped a little. 'Oh!' She was certainly surprised, but secretly pleased to hear his news. 'You like it that much, do you?'

'Sure. It's a great country. I like the folks I work with, I like my apartment, and I love the way of life and the sun.' Craig paused, covering her hand with his. 'I know you wouldn't consider it when I first went out, but how about now I've paved the way? Any second thoughts? You'd have no problems. They love English nurses, and you've got all the relevant experience.'

She drew a long breath as she shook her head. 'You make it sound absolutely wonderful, but it's not for me, Craig. Sorry. I'd be homesick in ten minutes flat.'

He screwed up a corner of his mouth. 'I kind of expected this. The thing is, where does it leave us?'

'Seems like the end of the line, doesn't it?' Fiona returned, after a moment.

Craig gave a brittle laugh. 'You don't sound exactly devastated. Have you met someone else?'

She half-heartedly smiled. 'No, but trying to carry on a love-affair with the Atlantic between us—well, it wasn't the best arrangement. I'm afraid I went off the boil some time ago. How about you? Be honest.'

'Oh, I loved receiving your mail. But as you say, it didn't help to further whatever it was we once had,' Craig admitted, albeit reluctantly.

Fiona was utterly relieved to hear him say so. 'Have you met somebody else?' she ventured.

His lips puckered. 'Well, I can't pretend I've been a plaster saint—but there's nobody special. Not as special as you could be if you'd agree to join me out there. Give it some more thought, won't you?'

'I'd rather we called it a day, really,' she said. 'No reason why we can't still be friends, Craig. Maybe I could come out for a holiday some time and you could show me around.'

He leaned across the table and kissed her. 'Do you have to be so sweet about it after I've kept you dangling? I could almost be persuaded to stay here if I weren't so hooked on the American lifestyle. I think I shall have to work on you.'

'Craig, if we'd been absolutely right for each other you couldn't have left me in the first place,' she pointed out, 'and I wouldn't need persuading. It was good while it lasted. Let's leave it at that.'

Accepting the truth of what she said, he let the matter rest. They fell to discussing his plans and the many friends he had to catch up with while he was in England.

'It's my brother's engagement party tomorrow,' Fiona

told him, 'and I was especially asked to say they'd love you to come, if your family can spare you.'

'Sure, I'd love to come,' Craig returned. 'My mother's arranged a family bash for Sunday, so that fits in rather nicely.'

Mindful that his family might be awaiting his arrival at his home in Chiswick, Fiona suggested it was time they were on their way. 'You ought to give your mum a call and let her know you've landed,' she prompted. 'If she's anything like mine she'll be on tenterhooks until she knows.'

'Mmm, I'll do that,' he said.

There was no mistaking the welcome when, in due course, they reached the road of modest semi-detached houses where Craig had grown up. Balloons and bunting festooned every available bush in the front garden.

'Hey, look at that,' he laughed. 'I didn't know I was so popular.'

'The prodigal son returns!' Fiona joshed, parking the car in the road outside.

His excited mother, watching from a window, threw open the front door and came running to greet him. She also hugged Fiona warmly and insisted that she stay to lunch. 'We were so grateful that you went to meet him,' she said. 'His dad's not too keen on that drive to Heathrow. Oh, don't you look well, son?'

It was a joyful reunion around the family table, at this stage with just his parents and themselves and a great deal of superficial talk. After lunch, however, Fiona decided to be diplomatic and make herself scarce.

'I'm sure you must have much to talk about, and I'll be seeing you tomorrow evening, Craig. It'll be a posh do, by the way,' she thought she had better say.

He grinned. 'OK, honey. I have got some decent gear with me. Thanks for the taxi service, and for—er—everything.' He saw her to the car, where they hugged and kissed affectionately. He hadn't yet told his parents he wasn't back for good.

'Are they going to be very disappointed?' she asked.

'Well, it's not that far,' he said, 'and I'll invite them out for a holiday.'

On a high with relief, Fiona drove back to Hampstead. The break had been easier than she'd anticipated. It inclined her to wonder if there *might* be another girl in the picture somewhere.

In a kind of celebration of her release she stopped at a florist shop in the town and bought the most extravagant armful of flowers for her prospective sister-in-law.

'Hi, Debs! I'm in here,' she called from the kitchen on hearing the other girl arrive home shortly afterwards. 'I'm putting the kettle on.'

Deborah's eyes were wide with surprise at finding Fiona there alone. 'Hello!' she said. 'Did you meet Craig all right? I thought. . .' Her eyes strayed to the bouquet on the table. 'Wow, they're gorgeous. From him?'

'No, from me to you,' Fiona beamed. 'I did intend to bring some with me yesterday, but the shops were shut.'

'My favourite colours!' Deborah drooled over the glorious mixture in shades of primrose to flame. 'It's awfully sweet of you, love. Thanks. But where's Craig, then?'

'In the bosom of his family. I took him home to Chiswick. And Debs,' Fiona pretended a long face, 'I've been dumped.'

'You've been *what*?' Deborah was astounded. 'Just like that? Well, he didn't hang about, did he?' She eyed Fiona uncertainly. 'H-how do you feel about it?'

Her guest broke into giggles. 'Ecstatic, really. As if I've been released from purdah. Now I can do what I like, see who I like, without feeling guilty. It was mutual, by the way, and we're still friends. He's coming to your party tomorrow and I'm going to their family party on Sunday, if you don't mind. Tea, is it?'

Deborah nodded, smiling as she stripped off her weatherproof jacket and draped it over the back of a chair. 'Can't say I'm surprised, only I thought it might take longer to happen. What brought things to a head?'

'The fact that he's not back to stay. He's going back to the States after Christmas, for another year. He tried to persuade me to join him, but he wasn't all that pressing. I did wonder. . .'

'If there's someone else over there?' Deborah finished for her.

'Mmm. Which made it simpler for me to pull out.' Fiona poured the tea. 'Oh, Debs, I feel so—free!' She whirled around the kitchen. 'Like a floating balloon. Something's bound to bring me down to earth before long.'

The other girl grinned. 'Positive thinking, now. This could be your opportunity for the start of the next great adventure.'

'Yes, that's the kind of thing Rory might say,' Fiona mused.

Beyond giving her a sideways glance, Deborah made no further comment on the matter. She searched a low cupboard for a suitable vase for her flowers, chose a large stone pitcher and began filling it with water.

'About tomorrow, anything I can do to help?' Fiona asked. 'Anything we can do tonight?'

'Nothing at all. James wouldn't let me do a thing.' While she talked, Deborah enjoyed arranging her assort-

ment of exotic blooms. 'He's booked caterers to do it all.
So tomorrow morning you and I are free to go clothes
shopping, if that's all right by you? James always has a
busy surgery on Saturday morning, so we don't have
him to consider.'

'Great,' Fiona agreed. 'Have you got some idea of
what you want?'

'Yes, I've been looking around bridal departments in
town, and I've seen something I rather like in one of the
Regent Street stores. There were some nice bridesmaid
dresses too. We're both stock size, luckily, so there
should be no problem.' Deborah stood back to admire
her arrangement. 'These will look lovely in the hall. Just
the job.'

'Am I to be the only bridesmaid?' Fiona asked.

'Yes, love. One's enough at my age,' Deborah
chuckled. 'Anyway, most of my friends are married and
in various stages of pregnancy.'

The two girls spent a happy hour browsing through
bridal magazines, discussing styles and colours.

Later, when James was home, there were equally vital
things to discuss, such as hymns for the service, and the
menu for the reception, and the vexed choice of guests.

Clowning, James clutched his brow. 'Decisions,
decisions! Nobody warned me what I was letting myself
in for. Shall we stay as we are, Debs?'

'Too late,' she cried. 'We've booked the church and
the organist is practising his party piece.'

Fiona gazed at them both fondly. 'You don't know
how lucky you are,' she said.

# CHAPTER SEVEN

On Saturday morning James drove Deborah and Fiona to the underground station before going on to his dental practice. 'Good shopping, you two, but don't be late back,' he warned. 'The caterers will be arriving around five o'clock.'

'I'll keep my eye on the time,' Fiona promised.

In excellent spirits, the girls bought their tickets and joined the throng of travellers for the short ride to London's West End. Alighting at Oxford Circus, they made for Regent Street, where Christmas decorations were already garlanding the wide thoroughfare. Shop window displays were also festive, with pantomime scenes and animated puppets delighting shoppers.

On reaching the exclusive fashion store where Deborah had already done a little browsing, they took the lift to the bridal department and looked among the wide selection of wedding dresses. After a great deal of debating over this one or that, Deborah now stepped from a changing cubicle for Fiona's approval. The gown she had on was an Empire-line model in flowing ivory crêpe de Chine, its flattering square neckline and full sleeves beaded with tiny seed pearls.

'What do you think?' she asked, her eyes bright.

Fiona caught her breath. 'Oh, that's the one. It's absolutely gorgeous.'

The mature shop assistant helping them added her approval. 'Lovely, madam, and a perfect fit.'

Bending to peer at the hemline of the softly textured

material, Fiona pointed out a dirty mark, but the assistant waved a dismissive hand. 'This is just a demonstration model. We would order specially for you, madam.'

'Oh, great.' Deborah gave a happy sigh. 'Will you do that, then, please?'

Her choice made and delivery promised in good time, they next looked among the bridesmaid dresses for Fiona. Avoiding some of the fussier models, a ballerina-length coral-pink dress with a cross-over bodice and cape-effect collar was at length decided upon, as making a pleasing contrast with Deborah's elegant outfit.

They next lingered among the enchanting display of bridal headdresses and hats, trying various models. But finally Deborah decided against, coming back to her original idea of fresh gardenias for her hair.

'But you have a hat, if you'd like one,' she offered.

Fiona also decided that she too would prefer flowers for her hair. There followed a belated lunch and a little more window-shopping. Then, with a feeling of satisfaction, they returned home to prepare for the evening festivities.

Fiona kicked off her boots in the kitchen while they relaxed over a cup of tea and looked at some of the toiletries they had bought. 'I really enjoyed today,' she said. 'There's a different feel about the West End. The air of opulence, I suppose.'

'More to your liking than yesterday's excursion, was it?' Deborah returned with a smile.

'You can say that again! Although the way things turned out, it was nowhere as difficult as I thought it might be.'

'Anticipation is often worse than the event. At least, that's what I always tell the patients,' said Deborah, laughing. 'So we won't be ordering a wedding dress for you this side of Christmas?'

'Not before *next* Christmas, either. Or the one after that,' Fiona declared. 'It's much less complicated being a career girl.'

Around fifty guests were expected from among James's professional circle and Deborah's hospital colleagues and mutual friends, but the house was quite large enough to accommodate them comfortably. Furniture was rearranged in the spacious open-plan living area. A large buffet table was put up along one wall, with a smaller table nearby holding drinks and glasses. With the caterers busying themselves in the kitchen, the family went up to their rooms to dress.

Fiona heard the doorbell ring as she prepared to slip into her new black cocktail frock. She heard her brother's cheery whistle as he skimmed downstairs to answer it. And she had no difficulty in recognising Rory's deep voice as the pair of them came back up the stairs. She found herself having to breathe very deeply, as though someone had punched all the air out of her. Sitting in front of the dressing-table mirror, it was as much as she could do to keep her hand steady while she applied her eye make-up. That man! He really did have the most irrational effect upon her when even his disembodied voice could put her in a state. Perhaps now that she had made one effort at applying for a sister's post she should try for another elsewhere. It would at least get him out of her life.

Emerging from her room a little later, Fiona came face to face with the man on her mind. Now dressed in a dinner-jacket, Rory came from his own room and they almost collided on the landing.

'Oh, hello!' He looked her over, his blue eyes approving. 'The sight of you alone has made my journey worthwhile.'

She bobbed him a curtsey, her own manner frivolous. 'Thank you, kind sir. That's what you should be saying to the bride-to-be, not to me.'

'I've done that. And I've told James what a lucky guy he is. It's a great thing when a couple are so right for each other as those two.' Rory paused, his arresting smile creating havoc in her breast. 'How did it go—your meeting with your friend?' he asked.

'Fine!' she said. 'He's coming tonight, so you'll be meeting him.'

'You look positively glowing,' he remarked. 'Is that because you fell in love with him all over again?'

To her annoyance she felt herself blushing. 'It's really a question of whether I do or don't want to work in the USA,' she returned evasively. 'That's where Craig's future lies. It might be worth considering, since I didn't get the sister's job you pressured me to apply for.' It was all a load of rubbish off the top of her head, but he wasn't to know that.

'Unfortunately, the other applicant did have a better claim, since she already had sister status,' he said. 'But you mustn't let one small setback influence your decision.'

Cheerful voices downstairs in the hall heralded the arrival of more guests, and among them she spotted Craig. 'I think we'd better go down,' she said, glad of the excuse to get away.

'So you're the guy her letters were full of,' Craig breezed, when introduced to Rory.

'What do you mean—*full of*?' Fiona laughingly protested. 'I might have mentioned him once or twice. I had to fill the pages up with something, didn't I?'

Since his travels Craig had become much more gregarious and he mixed freely with everyone, pleased to find an interested audience when talking about the differences between English and American health care. In fact, on the whole Fiona saw no more of him than anyone else while she also mixed and made herself agreeable to other guests.

Deborah's parents were among the visitors, and during the evening her father made a touching tribute to his daughter and James. It occured to Fiona that there would be no real father to give her this kind of support if or whenever she contemplated marriage. Of course, there was always James, and she couldn't wish for a more considerate brother, but it wasn't quite the same. . .

It so happened that Rory was at her elbow as everyone raised their glasses to the happy couple. Covertly she brushed away a threatening tear.

'What's the matter with you?' he murmured in her ear.

Fiona smiled up at him. 'Just feeling sentimental. It was a nice speech, wasn't it?'

He laid an arm around her shoulders. 'Just so long as it's not this business of Craig going back to America that's troubling you.'

'No, just the usual jumble of feelings one gets before weddings. Although since James and Debs have been living together already, things won't be quite that different for them.'

Rory nodded in agreement, his arm still around her shoulders.

She would never understand what prompted her to

raise the subject of his past, unless it was that, being surrounded by people whom they both knew only slightly, they were as good as alone.

'You were going to be married once, weren't you?' she said.

For a moment he was silent, his mouth tightening. Then, 'Yes,' he said, 'until circumstances decided otherwise. James told you, did he?'

She nodded. 'I'm sorry. Life's a pig sometimes, isn't it?'

He let out a long sigh. 'Time heals, Effie. That old chestnut we trot out so glibly to other people—it *is* true. The days pass, and you wake up one morning and the sun's shining and you realise that life is good. But what a morbid subject for a happy occasion.' He smiled and dropped a kiss on the top of her head. 'Can I get you some more bubbly?'

The tension building inside her was at bursting point. She didn't want his light, throwaway kisses. She wanted a wild, unrestrained meeting of their mouths. That, and much more. Her eyes strayed across the room to where Craig was chatting with someone else, and she wished he would come to her rescue. All the evening she had been overly conscious of Rory's presence. How was it that, whoever she was with or he was with, when she glanced his way their eyes had somehow happened to meet? Now James was putting on some dance music, and she knew she couldn't bear to be in his arms if Rory asked her to dance.

'No, I've had enough to drink,' she said. 'Excuse me, I'd better go and talk to Craig or he'll accuse me of neglecting him.'

The evening wound slowly to its close. The caterers

cleaned up and departed and the guests began to leave. At last there was only Craig, Rory and themselves left.

'Like some coffee with us before you go, Craig?' Deborah invited.

'Thanks, that would be nice,' he said.

So there they were, the five of them. Deborah and James side by side on the sofa, Craig and Rory sitting opposite each other and exchanging weighing-up-type glances, and Fiona seated on the carpet propped against her brother's knees.

She wished Craig would decide to leave soon so that she could go to bed, but everyone seemed glued to their chairs and thoroughly relaxed and talkative. When Rory actually got around to telling the others how she had neatly stitched up a convict earlier that week, Fiona was acutely embarrassed.

The soft lamplight shining on her blonde hair created an aureole around her piquant features.

'To look at her,' Rory pointed out teasingly, 'you'd think she'd pass out at the sight of blood, wouldn't you?'

'For goodness' sake!' Fiona protested, 'I'm not that fragile. And he was only a mixed-up guy who was down on his luck.'

'Who happened to have stuck a knife into his girl-friend's innards,' the consultant said, mildly. 'It was probably as well you didn't know that.'

'Fiona's OK. She's got what it takes,' Craig declared with a warm smile.

'And as of now if I don't go to bed soon I shall flake out,' she warned. 'I suppose you *are* planning to go home tonight, Craig?'

'If you insist,' he drawled.

He said his farewells and Fiona went to the front door to see him off. He took her in his arms. 'Tomorrow evening, then, around seven, at Chiswick?' he said. "Bye, honey.'

They kissed affectionately, but she felt no desire to prolong the parting. She felt nothing at all beyond friendship, whereas Craig hugged her closely and murmured, 'Promise me you'll have another think about coming out to me? I know you'd love it.'

'I will think,' she said, 'but I'm pretty sure it's not for me.'

'I can probably guess why. Don't try to kid me it's because you've got Britain stamped across your heart,' he returned sarcastically, brushing a last kiss across her mouth.

'Oh, I hate people who talk in riddles. Go home,' she said.

Waving him goodbye as he drove off, she called goodnight to the others and went upstairs to her room. She assumed Craig's innuendo was directed at Rory, but how could he have guessed how she felt about the consultant? She had tried really hard to stay cool whenever she was in Rory's company.

It was true you could often tell when people were attracted to each other. There was that certain zing in the air, like that between Debs and James. You only had to catch a glimpse of the passing touch to know how things were between those two. But between Rory and herself? No, Craig was just trying to dream up a reason for her refusal to go along with him.

She heard the others come up to bed, and she heard the hall clock chiming every quarter-hour to two a.m. With sleep seeming impossible she put on her robe and crept downstairs to make a drink. There was light coming from the living-room. Assuming that James had forgotten to switch it off, Fiona went in to do so. And she jumped as her startled eyes met Rory's. In a Paisley silk dressing-gown, his dark hair rumpled, he was stretched in an easy-chair reading a newspaper.

'Hi!' he murmured in surprise. 'You're not sleep walking, are you?'

Her heart thudding, she smiled and whispered back, 'No. . . I was thirsty. Came down for a drink. What are you doing up?'

'Couldn't sleep. I'm not used to clocks chiming all through the night.'

He followed her into the kitchen, where she took some milk from the fridge. 'Can I make you a drink?'

'No, thanks. I had some whisky—I hope James won't mind.'

'Of course he won't.' She warmed her milk in the microwave, very conscious of her own rumpled appearance as he watched her across the table.

He was sitting astride a chair, resting his arms along the back and his square chin on his arms. 'Craig seems a nice guy,' he said suddenly.

'Of course. I only go for nice guys,' she joked.

'But not enough to follow him overseas, I hope?'

Cupping the mug in her hands, Fiona sipped her drink. 'Why do you hope?'

His eyes were impish. 'We-ell, we can't have the best of our nurses deserting us, can we?'

'Oh, I'm the best now, am I? That makes a nice change.' She drank her milk, looking at him as she finished it. 'We could stop the clock, if it's disturbing you.'

'It wasn't really the clock,' he confessed with a half-smile. 'Things on my mind. Better not interfere with the works or it might rouse the others. Are you ready to go up now?'

She nodded, put her mug in the sink and went ahead of him quietly up the stairs. Outside her room she turned to murmur goodnight.

He leaned towards her, one arm around her waist. Without knowing quite how it happened she found their lips meeting. But what began as a social kiss became more prolonged and startlingly intimate. By mutual accord, or so she felt, their kiss deepened, like the wild and ecstatic union she had longed for earlier. Her heart raced as Rory's embrace tightened and her mouth opened for his. But suddenly he put her from him. Drawing a deep breath and looking a little awkward, with a whispered, 'Goodnight!' he left her.

Acutely embarrassed, Fiona fled into her own room, dismayed at what he might now have guessed.

It had gone nine before Fiona stirred the following morning, after a fitful night. She lay for a moment watching sunlight filtering through the chintzy curtains, trying to collect her thoughts about the events of the previous night. Had she made an awful fool of herself, or would Rory dismiss their nocturnal interlude as an excess of partytime spirits? That would be the best way to handle it, she thought. She had only to get through today and by the time they were back at the hospital it would all fade into the background. In Rory's opinion she was harebrained anyway, so it was all in character.

Screwing her pale gold locks on top of her head, she had a restorative soak in the bath, dressed in jeans and a thigh-length cyclamen sweater and wandered downstairs looking dewy-fresh.

In the kitchen the others were gathered around the breakfast table, lingering over coffee.

'And about time too!' her brother said.

'Good morning, all,' Fiona returned cheerfully. 'How's everyone?' She directed her remarks to James and Deborah, not daring to look in Rory's direction.

'Everyone's fine. At least, the chaps seem to be.' Deborah pushed lazy fingers through her dark hair. 'I'm still recovering. How about you?'

Somehow Fiona knew instinctively that Rory had said nothing to the others about their meeting in the small hours. 'Yes, I'm OK.' Seating herself at the table, she watched while Deborah poured her some coffee. 'Great party. You should get engaged more often,' she joked.

'Your turn next, Eff,' James put in. 'But let's get over the wedding first. Now what's all this I was hearing from Craig about you following his example and making tracks for the USA?'

Fiona shook her head. 'I fobbed him off with a promise to think about it. But what would the great British public do without me?'

Rory, who had said nothing until then, now remarked drily, 'Much the same as they did without me, I imagine.'

She helped herself to cornflakes, casting him an impudent glance. 'Come on! You're supposed to say something like— *What indeed*! But then, I should know by now, compliments from *you* are like manna from heaven.'

'At least they're not cheap. When you get one you know you've earned it,' he replied.

Her brother looked askance from one to the other. 'Well, it's a glorious morning. I think what we all need is a nice long walk on the Heath to blow the cobwebs away. Then we could have a pub lunch somewhere. All in favour?'

The suggestion was greeted with approval, and within the next half hour, suitably clad in trainers and jackets, the four of them were enjoying the autumnal beauty of Hampstead's rustic heathland. With leaves rustling beneath their feet and many of the trees still in their glowing autumn foliage, it was impossible not to feel uplifted.

To begin with Fiona strolled with Deborah, talking weddings, while the two men kept each other company. Later she found herself with James while Rory and Deborah fell into step. Chatting with her brother, Fiona recalled how the Heath reminded her of her training years, when she used to stay with him on her days off.

'It was fun most of the time, except that I was scared stiff of registrars, let alone consultants. That all seems centuries ago now. . .'

'And you can be rude to Rory with impunity,' James observed with a grin.

'I never am,' she argued. 'I only retaliate when he deserves it. That man can be a real dour Scot when it suits him.'

Her brother laughed. 'He's had a rough time, remember. But he's mellowing.'

They stopped for a time to watch a grey squirrel skimming up a tree trunk and to gaze at the misty view of the City's skyline in the distance. Then it was on towards one of the ponds, where Fiona paused again, amused by the sight of some mallards making a splash as they up-ended their tails. Looking around to make a comment on the rural scene, she unexpectedly found herself alone with Rory; something she had been doing her best to avoid.

'Oh, it's you,' she said. 'Grand, isn't it? Only a stone's throw from the West End, and it seems as if we're in the country.'

'Yes.' Rory smiled down at her, and there was a

certain something in the smile which made her colour rise.

He pointed away across the water to where an angler was casting his line. 'Let's hope that guy over there doesn't end up with a fishhook in his finger,' he said.

'If he does it'll let him know what it feels like to be a fish,' she returned.

They began to walk on together, Rory slowing his pace to her smaller steps, putting out a hand when she stumbled over a rut in the grass.

'I had an odd dream last night,' he mentioned casually, looking into the distance. 'I was wandering around in a strange house when, from out of nowhere, a seductive young lass in a pink housecoat came up to me, and we kissed.'

A breeze blew her hair across Fiona's face and she lifted it back. 'How extraordinary,' she returned, joining in the game, although her pulse was stampeding. 'You dream in colour, do you? Was it a pleasant experience?'

His lips twitched. 'Absolutely delightful. I'm sorry not to be spending another night here. I might have hoped for a repeat experience.'

She chose to ignore his teasing. 'When are you going back?' she asked.

'After lunch. I've got a dinner date with Pat Green and his wife tonight.'

'Dr Green. He's nice,' Fiona enthused. 'But then so are most paediatricians, I find.'

'As against an orthopaedic surgeon, who might not warrant such glowing terms?'

She wrinkled her nose at him. 'The thought never crossed my mind.'

'And what are your plans for the rest of the day?'

'I'm committed to going to Chiswick,' Fiona sighed.

'Craig's parents have invited hordes of their relatives. I shall probably feel completely out of it, or get pestered to say what are our plans for the future. I'm not looking forward to it much.'

'Then why ever did you agree to go?'

'We-ell,' she shrugged impatiently, 'it would have looked odd not to. We haven't had a great row or anything, and we are good mates. I didn't want to bring a sour note into his first weekend back.'

Rory screwed up a corner of his mouth. 'Noble sentiments, but sometimes the sharpest cut is kindest. Unless, of course, you still hanker to keep things alive between you.'

'Oh, no, I don't. If I were—if *we* were madly in love or anything I'd want to go wherever he went, wouldn't I? But we're not, although he might fancy whipping it up into something. So that's that, and I know what I'm doing.'

'If only I were ten years younger,' he murmured.

Fiona gave a quick sideways glance, assuming he was again teasing, but there was no trace of a smile in his enigmatic expression.

'Why, what difference would that make?' she asked.

For answer he caught her hand and said, 'Come on, we ought to catch up with the others.'

They walked on in silence in the brilliant sunshine, and Fiona's head was full of questions which she dared not ask. Did he mean that if he were ten years younger he might have been interested in her himself? But what difference did a few years make? Either you were physically drawn to someone or you weren't. And Fiona wanted Rory so badly that she could scarcely conceal her feelings. Maybe what he said was just an idle figure of speech—the sort of thing older men sometimes said to younger girls, not really meaning it. But she wondered—and she had to know.

Presently she said, in a light-hearted way, her long-lashed eyes raised to his, 'So what difference would it make, Rory, if there were no age-gap between us? Would you fancy me?'

He squeezed her hand. 'I'll forget you asked me that, Effie. Don't flirt with me. You're an adorable girl, but I'm too old for you.' He laughed. 'For goodness' sake, lass, before Craig's out of sight you'll have other young guys queueing up whose hearts you can break. You can't have mine as well.'

They had by now caught up with James and Deborah, which brought a timely end to the subject which Fiona could have bitten her tongue for starting. He might have meant what he said kindly, but she had never felt so embarrassed.

Nearby was James's car where they had left it, and a short drive brought them to the Spaniards Inn for their lunch.

The mildness of the day made it possible to have their food alfresco-style at a table in the garden, and on the face of it there couldn't have been a merrier group. James and Deborah were full of their plans for the future. Rory was his most charming self, comparing the joys of English life with his experiences in Bangladesh, and Fiona staged a good impression of being cheerful and carefree.

Inwardly, however, and sitting within touching distance of Rory on the same wooden bench, Fiona could have wept. Why couldn't he believe that the years between them were of no consequence at all? Unless, and it was possible, he didn't happen to feel towards her the same as she felt for him. But there *was* an indefinable something between them. She knew it. And if the pull was so strong for her, surely he must feel it too? Well, she would just have to let things take their course and hope that one day. . . Failing that, she would probably stay single for the rest of her life, Fiona brooded. Anyone else could only be second best.

Back at the house Rory went up to his room to pack and they all had a last few words together in the drive before he set off.

'Good to have you within spitting distance again, old chum,' James said, shaking his friend warmly by the hand. 'I suppose we shan't see you again before the wedding?'

'I doubt it,' Rory said. 'Some time between now and then I have to make it to Edinburgh to see my mother, or she'll be disowning me.' He hugged Deborah and gave her a kiss. 'Thanks for a great weekend—I really enjoyed it.' Turning to Fiona, he said, 'A pity we couldn't have travelled together, but maybe next time, eh?'

'Yes, I'll let you drive me up to the wedding,' she promised.

He planted a light kiss on her lips, holding both her hands in his. 'Drive carefully tomorrow. We want you back at the Memorial in one piece, remember.'

'I didn't know you cared,' she bantered.

Playfully he ruffled her hair, then stepped into his car and they waved him out of sight.

'Not once did he mention Corinne,' James said thoughtfully. 'I reckon he must have come to terms. Is there anyone else on the horizon, Eff, do you know?'

'How should I know?' she retorted. 'I only work with him.'

'Yes, but in hospital life everyone knows who's seeing whom. Or they did in my young days.'

'James, stop badgering your sister,' Deborah said with a half-smile. 'Sometimes I think you've got cloth between your ears.'

'Why, what have I said?' he demanded. 'What's she on about, Eff?'

Fiona spread her hands and laughed as they trooped back into the house. 'Beats me. Just don't expect me to keep tabs on your mate, that's all.'

'Let's have some tea. I'll put the kettle on.' Deborah made for the kitchen, and Fiona followed her while James went in search of the *Sunday Times*.

'You've guessed, haven't you, Debs?' Fiona sighed. 'Is it so obvious?'

'You mean you're in love with Rory—or you think you are? Well, he is rather gorgeous,' Deborah admitted, 'and you are between romances. Don't worry, I won't say anything to James.'

'Thanks,' Fiona breathed. 'Maybe I'll get over it. Do you think the age difference matters? It's only eleven years.'

Deborah smiled sympathetically. 'I'm not passing any opinion. It's really a question of attitude. There's James at thirty-four, and sometimes he's as daft as a schoolboy.'

'Who are you talking about?' James asked, catching the tail-end of the remark.

'Mind your own business. This is girl-talk.' Deborah blew him a kiss and exchanged a conspiratorial smile with Fiona.

# CHAPTER EIGHT

SHORTLY after nine o'clock the following morning Deborah came into Fiona's room with a mug of coffee.

'Wakey, wakey!' she said.

Fiona heaved herself up against the pillows, stretching pleasurably. 'Thanks, Debs. You spoil me.'

Perching on the side of the bed, Deborah settled down to hear how her future sister-in-law had fared the previous night. 'Didn't hear you come home. We went to bed early. How was the party at Craig's place?'

'Every bit as boring as I thought it might be.' Fiona sipped her drink. 'No, that's not fair, really,' she corrected. 'They were all terribly nice to me, especially Craig's mum and dad. The truth is, I felt a bit of an imposter, knowing that things are more or less over between us. He hasn't told anyone about that yet.'

'And it wouldn't surprise me if your mind was on someone else,' Deborah remarked intuitively.

A whimsical smile lit Fiona's eyes. 'Meaning Rory? Well, yes, it was now and then.'

'Don't let yourself get paranoid about him,' the older girl advised. 'I'll admit he terribly attractive. But there's plenty more fish in the sea. And you've got a lot going for you too, Eff. You can afford to take your time and be choosy.'

Fiona rubbed her nose with the back of her hand. 'Yes, I know you're right. It's probably because he seems to be out of reach that I fancy him. Don't worry about me. It's just a passing crush.'

'Fine. 'Scuse me talking to you like your grandmother,' Deborah said with a soft laugh, 'only I've met these dedicated types, and I should hate to see you get hurt. Rory's very wrapped up in his work. I'd be surprised if he had much interest in romance at present.'

'Mmm, you may be right,' Fiona mused. 'That's what I'm going to become, a dedicated type,' she said. 'From now on men are going to take a back seat in my life. For amusement only.'

Deborah grinned. 'Until the next time! How about Craig—are you seeing any more of him before you go back?'

'No, not this time. He's got some friends he wants to look up. He may come up to see me on my next days off, but that won't be for another ten days after this lot. James already gone to the surgery, has he?' Fiona asked.

'Yes, he always starts early. It's a busy practice. He said goodbye to you and advised not to leave it late before you go back. It's raining hard—could be nasty on the motorway.'

Fiona glanced towards the window and the lowering sky beyond and groaned. 'Oh, blow! I did think we might have a mooch around the local shops this morning, but there's no fun paddling around in the rain. And you're on at one, aren't you?' Deborah nodded, and Fiona went on, 'Well, I'll have an early lunch with you and then get on my way. No sense in hanging about, is there?'

At midday the two girls sat down to some sandwiches and coffee, then Deborah set off for work at the nearby hospital, leaving Fiona to finish her packing and see herself off on the journey back to Berkshire.

It was sensible, she had to agree, travelling back in daylight, weather conditions being what they were. In fact they seemed to have worsened since the morning. Her windscreen wipers were having to work at the double to clear a view through the driving rain.

She stopped to take in petrol before getting on to the motorway, and while she filled up her thoughts wandered back over the past few days. It had been a strange kind of weekend, with Craig's homecoming overlapping their own family celebrations, and her being thrust into the consultant's company because of it. She was glad it was over, although she had enjoyed the shopping. But London held no real charms for her now and she was happy to be going back to her own way of life. She tried to ignore the small traitorous voice inside her which pointed out that this was because every mile she drove brought her nearer to Rory—the man she was intent on doing her best to disregard. Unfortunately he would keep coming into her head.

Fiona sighed heavily as she replaced her petrol cap and went to pay the bill. Oh, well, even if Rory declined to see her in a romantic light, there was no reason why she shouldn't enjoy the special relationship which his friendship with James extended to her. The trouble was she didn't think she could bear it if he should start dating someone else.

Once on the motorway she was too occupied to think about anything else but watching the road. Headlights glistened on the wet black surfaces and at intervals hazard lights flashed, warning drivers to reduce speed. But even with the appalling weather conditions some of the passing traffic flashed by in the fast lane, unconcerned. High-sided commercial lorries swishing past Fiona's small car in an alarming fashion threw up filthy spray to cloud her windscreen.

Some two hours later she arrived back at Sycamore

Grange, relieved that the journey was over. As she let herself into the house, the first person she met was Lois, coming from the laundry-room with some freshly ironed uniforms over her arm.

'Hi!' Lois greeted her. 'You're back early. Had a good time?'

'Yes, great, apart from the drive home. That was horrendous. The way some of those Continental trucks thunder along is enough to scare the hell out of you.'

They went up the stairs together, Fiona lugging her suitcase which she dumped down outside her door while she sorted out her room key from the bunch.

'Come over to me when you've parked your gear,' Lois invited. 'I'll make coffee and you can tell me what you got up to.'

Having discarded her damp jacket and boots, Fiona slipped her feet into comfortable sheepskin moccasins and padded across the corridor to her friend. 'Were you working this morning?' she asked.

'Yeah. I was called down to A and E to help out with Rory's minor injuries clinic, as a matter of fact. Someone phoned in sick.' Lois put her feet up on the sofa and cupped her drink in her hands. 'I enjoyed it—made a nice change from the ward routine. Well, come on,' she pressed, 'what was it like living in the same house with the boss? Did you get matey? I mean, he's great to work with, but I'm still a bit in awe of him. Whereas you probably saw him in his pyjamas—if he wears them,' she giggled.

Fiona smiled to herself, remembering their solitary small-hours encounter. 'He's OK,' she said non-committally. 'Quite normal, really. We did the ordinary things, in a foursome, like going for a tramp on the Heath and watching the ducks and having a pub lunch, et cetera.

But I don't think I penetrated too far beneath his shell.' She wanted to get off the subject of Rory, so she talked about Craig instead. 'We've at last agreed to pack it in. He's not coming back to England and I don't want to go over there—so it's curtains. You've no idea what a weight that is off my mind,' she said. 'I'm now a completely free woman!'

'I'm amazed you didn't call it off before,' Lois declared. 'There was nothing to stop you dating anyone else if you'd wanted to.'

'I know. The truth is, I hadn't met anyone else who interested me that much,' Fiona confessed. She went on to enthuse about her shopping spree with Deborah, describing the wedding clothes they had ordered. 'Everything's geared for Christmas already, up in the West End,' she said. 'The window displays are fantastic, but it was a bit much to have carols playing over the loudspeakers this early.'

'They'll probably be asking for volunteers to sing carols around the wards here before long,' Lois was saying, when her telephone rang.

Watching her amble over to answer it, Fiona saw the other girl's customary bright expression fade. Her face blanched.

'A yellow alert? Oh, my God!' she exclaimed, pushing back her long brown hair. 'Yes—yes—Fiona's here with me. OK, we'll come.' Laying down the receiver, Lois stood there as if pole-axed, her eyes wide with dismay. She gulped. 'That was Sister Fuller. There's been a major incident on the motorway, and we're the main receiving unit!'

Equally alarmed, Fiona had already sprung to her feet. 'Come on,' she urged, running for the door, 'we'd better get into uniform. We can take my car—I haven't put it away. Anyone else we ought to tell?'

'Yes—the girls downstairs. Upstairs are both working already,' Lois returned, wriggling out of her jeans.

Dashing down the stairs, Fiona passed the message on to the two ground-floor residents, then raced back up again to get herself changed, stuffing the necessary equipment of scissors, pencil torch, stethoscope and pens into her pockets.

Within ten minutes they were on their way, driving through the rain with only hazy ideas of what awaited them. Although the hospital had a clear-cut policy for large-scale disasters and from time to time had a practice run, it was the thing they all dreaded. Some of the staff at the Memorial had been involved in other such incidents, but for Fiona and Lois this was a first.

They talked nervously on the way. It was four o'clock and the light was beginning to fade.

Fiona said, 'I don't envy the ambulance crews and the police, sorting out the chaos in this weather. Did they say how many vehicles were involved?'

'I think Anna mentioned fifty, but I wasn't registering properly.' Lois chewed her thumbnail. 'She was on about emptying one of our wards to put all the casualties together.'

'I hope Molly's in control in A and E,' said Fiona. 'She doesn't flap. But it'll be much the same as any of the RTAs we deal with, I suppose, only more of them.'

Afterwards Fiona could never remember parking the car and the initial tasks like clearing the department of non-urgent cases. Her main impression was of the number of white-coated doctors everywhere, from every specialty, and nurses from other wards who had been sent down to help, and off-duty staff coming from wherever they happened to be, and the constant passage of wheelchairs and stretchers.

While Lois went straight to her own ward Fiona reported to Casualty. And she was more than glad to find that Molly Bland was on duty, appearing to be her usual unruffled self.

'Fiona!' Molly exclaimed. 'I didn't think you'd be back yet. Thanks for coming in. We've got plenty of help, but it's our own staff who are most useful—they know where everything is. Now, will you make sure that all the cubicles are properly equipped, and a couple of nurses at each if possible? Then you can help me triage with the doctors as cases arrive. I expect mostly minor injuries to begin with—it takes a time to get people out who are trapped in the wreckage. Kinross has gone off with the flying squad to help.'

Glad to have something to do, Fiona checked all the cubicles as directed and then went to meet the first ambulance with Adrian. Most of the eight people it brought were shocked, cold and wet. Some were very quiet, others gabbling on about the articulated lorry which had crashed through the central reservation, overturning and spilling its load of paper bales.

An elderly man holding a large pad of dressing over a gash on his forehead said he thought there had been a car travelling in the wrong direction which had started the pile up.

'It's carnage out there,' he pronounced. 'Everyone was travelling too fast. But those ambulance people, they're bloody marvellous.'

Wheelchairs were organised for those in need and the patients led away to be tagged with names and numbers and processed through for treatment, admission or discharge.

Fiona received a large-eyed little girl with muddied abrasions down one side of her face and a bandaged knee.

'Hello, darling.' She put her arm around the child and gave her a kindly smile. 'What's your name?'

'Wendy Turner,' was the tremulous reply.

Fiona didn't recall any adult by that name in the first batch of patients. 'Who were you travelling with, Wendy?'

'My mum and Uncle Terry.' The little girl's lips quivered. 'I fell out when our car bashed into the other one, and I couldn't find them afterwards. A policeman said they'd be coming here later.'

One of the ambulance crew raised her eyebrows at Fiona and imperceptibly shook her head. 'Perhaps they'll be along in the next ambulance, love,' she said in a cheerful voice.

'All right, Wendy, let's give you a ride in a wheel-chair,' Adrian said. 'We'll find a couple of nice nurses to look after you while you're waiting, eh?'

'Can you tell us any more about her?' Fiona asked in a private word with the ambulance driver when the child was out of earshot.

'We think she must have been KO'd. We found her dazed on the hard shoulder. She was lucky to be thrown clear. Most of the cars in that spot were a tangled wreck and nobody we spoke to seemed to know her. The police are aware she's been brought here alone.'

'OK, I'll put our social worker in the picture,' Molly promised when Fiona explained the child's predicament. 'In any case, we shall be keeping her overnight if they think she was knocked out.'

Another ambulance arrived, this time with two severely injured patients. One, an eight months pregnant woman, was deeply unconscious. She was rushed through to Resus to be seen by the neurological consultant and then prepared for an emergency Caesarean section. The other was a girl with a shattered pelvis who was also taken to Resus to be stabilised before the necessary surgery could begin.

And the casualties continued to filter through, during which time the staff worked steadily, all co-operating as a team. Fiona had no idea of the time as she helped sort out life-threatening cases from those which could wait a little. She produced equipment and drugs and antitetanus serum and provided packs of cross-matched blood as required.

There was no panic. Even the blasé Damien rose to the occasion like everyone else. Helpful policemen answered enquiries from the public and referred too-intrusive journalists to the hospital Press officer. And in the large day ward set aside for ambulant patients who had received treatment, reviving cups of tea were served by the sympathetic kitchen staff. Some of the patients were far from home, had lost possessions, and would be in need of help from the community services before being able to continue their journey.

It was eight o'clock before the department began to empty, by which time four people had gone straight to Theatre and twenty others had been warded pending further investigation. In the screened-off area which had been turned into a make-shift mortuary six bodies lay waiting to be identified, and the need for compassion for dealing with survivors drained even the strongest of the staff.

'Last patient coming in now,' Molly reported after receiving a telephone message. 'Girl with a fractured spine. She was pinned under one of the cars—Rory's coming with her. Fiona, tell the orthopaedic reg, will you, and you can handle this one right through now?'

With a jumble of feelings, Fiona sought out Dr Imran Singh, who was fitting a surgical collar to a man with a whiplash neck injury. 'There's a spinal injury on the way if you can come, please,' she said quietly. He nodded, and she went off to collect a trolley with X-ray facility. It crossed her mind that this patient might revive for Rory all the painful memories he thought were behind him. He could be back to square one.

Imran joined her at the ambulance entrance, rubbing a weary hand over his face. 'How many more?' he queried.

Fiona rested one tired foot behind the other. 'Molly said this one would be the last.'

The ambulance drew in, blue lights flashing. They went forward to meet it as the crew jumped down to open the doors. Rory came into view, clad in yellow fluorescent jacket and trousers, carefully supervising every movement of his dark-haired young patient. Fiona suddenly caught his eye, and for a moment visible relief flooded his controlled features.

'Oh, you're back!' he exclaimed. Then quickly turned to address his registrar. 'Fractures of the second or third lumbar vertebrae, I suspect, Imran. She's paraplegic. I've given methylprednisolone IM to reduce inflammation, which may be the cause of the paralysis. And she's had pethidine 100-mgs. X-ray, please. I may need to operate, and as soon as possible.' Leaning over the girl, he stroked her ashen cheek. 'I'll be seeing you again presently, Marie.' Then he strode off to get out of his waterproofs, leaving the others to follow their routine procedures.

The nineteen-year-old was pale and traumatised,

although luckily her face had escaped with a few bruises. She was already connected to a dextrose-saline drip.

'Not hurting too much at the moment, are you?' Fiona asked gently, holding the girl's hand as they wheeled her along to Resus.

Marie let out a sighing breath. 'No—but my legs won't move—and I can't feel them.' A look of panic filled her eyes. 'A-am I going to be—paralysed?' The tears brimmed over and trickled down her pallid cheeks.

'Well, we won't start imagining the worst before we see exactly what the problem is,' Imran said briskly. 'Were you travelling on your own?'

'Yes,' the girl murmured. 'I was going back to Oxford.'

In the resuscitation-room Fiona, with the help of another nurse, cut off the girl's jeans and sweatshirt and got her into an examination gown.

Imran asked questions while they worked, then made his own preliminary examination. 'Right,' he said, after recording her vital signs, 'X-ray next.' He phoned the radiographer to bring the portable machine.

By the time the X-ray plates were processed Rory had reappeared. Studying the films on the lighted viewing screen, the doctors discussed the results. It was as the consultant had originally surmised, the crushed vertebrae compressing the spinal cord. 'Yes, it'll have to be a laminectomy,' Rory said.

Going back to the patient, Rory took her hand between his. 'We need to operate, Marie. There are a couple of fractured vertebrae which will require plating. I can't make any promises as to the outcome, but, when the swelling goes down, let's hope you'll get some feeling back into these legs.' He smiled encouragingly. 'We'll do our best for you, lassie.'

The doctors left to make their preparations. Presently, having promised to make sure that Marie's parents were informed, Fiona wheeled her charge along to the operating theatre and left her in the hands of the theatre staff.

Pushing her tired limbs, she went back to the office to give Molly the phone number for Marie's parents and to see what else remained to be done.

'Nothing more for you, Fiona. The regular night staff can take over now and do the tidying up.' Molly passed a weary hand over her forehead. 'There's coffee outside. Do go and have some. Then the SNO wants to have a few words with everyone before you all leave.'

'Oh, right. I must wash my hands first.'

Like most people, Fiona had barely stopped since she arrived, and now that there was nothing more for her to do she felt lost and aimless. Stripping off her plastic apron, she made for the cloakroom. And there she met Aileen, her eyes red with tears.

'Aileen, what is it? What's the matter?' Fiona asked.

A fresh burst of convulsive sobbing shook the other girl before she could reply. 'O-oh, I'm just being daft. There was this man—he looked something like my dad. It wasn't, of course. Only h-he didn't make it. His chest was crushed,' she got out disjointedly. 'Oh, God! I'm not cut out for this job, Fiona. I was useless. I never know what to say to people—not like you. I *hate* it,' she went on stormily. 'I'll have to get a transfer. Or I might even leave.'

'Hey, come on,' Fiona said gently. She swallowed against the lump in her own throat. 'You did a good job out there—I know you did. We all felt inadequate, but we did what we could.' She handed Aileen some tissues. 'It's over for us now, anyway. Come and have some coffee.' With her arm linked through the other girl's she encouraged her out to join the other nurses about to finish work at last.

The senior nursing officer thanked everyone for their efforts, saying she had been really proud of the way the hospital had coped. 'In three and a half hours we've dealt with sixty-three casualties. The police have set up a casualty information bureau in the main entrance hall, so there'll be no need for any of you to deal with things like that. You've done your part. Later we shall have a proper debriefing session so that you can talk about your feelings in this matter. But for the moment, go home and try to rest. Many of you will be needed to staff the hospital tomorrow.'

Nobody seemed in a hurry to leave. It was almost as if they were in a dream world. They had all been stunned by the outcome of the motorway madness.

Fiona brought some coffee to Aileen and sat her down. She was relieved to hear that her erstwhile adversary lived in a bed-sit with another girl. 'Just so long as you won't be on your own,' she said.

Lois came down from where she had been looking after patients on the reception ward. They went home together and sat drinking hot chocolate in Fiona's flat, thinking about the various patients who had gone through their hands.

'What about that little girl, Wendy?' Fiona asked. 'Did the police get her tied up with her parents?'

'Yes,' Lois returned flatly. 'Her mother's lying in the mortuary.'

Fiona's eyes filled with tears. 'Oh, poor kid.'

'Fortunately she still has a father,' Lois went on. 'He lives in Oxford. Mum and the boyfriend had just collected Wendy after she'd been staying with him.'

\* \* \*

It was past ten o'clock when Lois decided to return to her own flat. 'I want to phone my mum, to let her know I wasn't on the motorway,' she said, after the late TV news had been flashing pictures of the horrors.

It reminded Fiona that she should telephone her brother and let him know she'd arrived safely. James and Deborah had been out and had only just heard news of the crash. 'I must have been just ahead of it all,' she told them, suddenly realising how nearly she might have been in the thick of it. 'Rory was having to operate on a girl with a fractured spine. It must be an awful reminder to him of what happened to his girlfriend,' she reflected.

'Well, being an orthopaedic surgeon he's bound to come up against things like that in his work,' James said bluntly. 'I expect he's learned to distance himself. Anyway, thanks for phoning, Eff. We were beginning to get alarmed.'

Fiona soaked her tired limbs in a fragrant bath, then took a good novel to bed with her in an attempt to push the events of the day out of mind, but it was hopeless trying to concentrate. She read the words, but they made no sense. Her own telephone ringing was a welcome relief. She climbed out of bed to answer it.

'Effie, sorry to disturb you at this late hour, but I had to check that it *was* you I saw in A and E this afternoon.'

The deep voice was almost like a caress, and her heart bounded madly. 'Yes, Rory, it was me,' she said. 'I know the whole thing seemed unreal, didn't it?'

'You must have come back very early.'

'I did. James thought it best because of the weather. Lucky, wasn't I? My guardian angel must have taken over,' she added with a shaky laugh.

'I was never more glad to see anyone in my life,' Rory admitted. 'There was a crunched-up white car in the middle of the mayhem. It could have been yours. You've no idea of the thoughts that ran through my head.'

He was silent for a moment, and so was she. Then he went on, 'Talk to me, Effie. I want to be convinced that this isn't part of the nightmare. Tell me what you were doing when I rang.'

She drew a tremulous breath. 'Well, I'd just gone to bed and I was trying to read, but not very successfully.' At a loss for what next to say, she took a cue from her brother, deciding that some things were best faced head-on. 'Tell me about the laminectomy—how did it go?' she asked. 'Were you able to. . .?'

'Yes, it went splendidly. So often one's worst fears are confirmed, but this time they weren't. Another reason why everything seems unreal, I expect. There was a blood clot pressing on the spinal cord. We were able to evacuate it, and we fixed the vertebrae. With average luck young Marie should get back the use of her legs before long.'

Fiona rejoiced with him. 'Rory, I'm so glad. It must be very rewarding.'

'Yes, it was. Made up for some of the problems we could do nothing about.' Again they were both silent until he went on, 'Well, I suppose I must let you go to sleep now. You've had a hard day. Thanks for talking to me.'

'You worked harder than anyone. Are you going to bed now?'

'At this moment I'm still at the hospital. There are some relatives to see, and some writing to do. But I'll be going soon. Will you be in tomorrow?'

'Yes, I'm on a late.'

'So I may see you around, then. Goodnight, Effie.'

'Goodnight,' she murmured, and waited until she heard the click of his phone before she put hers down.

Wonderingly she crawled back between the sheets, her thoughts in a whirl. He had cared enough to let her know he had been worried for her safety. And what did that mean? Was it the normal concern one might feel for a friend, or had he felt a tug at his heartstrings?

Today life had demonstrated forcibly that no one could count on tomorrow. How many of those casualties on the road this afternoon could have imagined themselves in such a life-and-death drama? And when the future was so uncertain, what did any amount of years between lovers matter?

She lay awake in the dark hoping that these same thoughts were in Rory's mind and that it would open his eyes to the truth that age was of no importance where love was concerned. She was his for the asking, and she had to try and show him that without being too obvious. The decision had to be his—or at least he had to think so.

# CHAPTER NINE

A WEEK had passed since that black Monday when the resources of the hospital had been stretched to the limit by the multiple road crash. No one had been untouched by the scale of the disaster. Everyone had his or her own private and painful memories; none more so than Fiona, who had been at the receiving end of so many of the casualties.

The plight of the little girl Wendy, whose mother had died, was brought vividly back to Fiona the following day when the child's father arrived and needed to be accompanied to the mortuary.

He broke down on identifying the body of his wife. 'We weren't divorced,' he told Fiona brokenly. 'She left me three months ago. I-I was still hoping. . .' He couldn't go on.

Fiona swallowed back the tears that pricked her own eyes. She laid a sympathetic hand on his arm. 'I'm so sorry,' she said.

Guiding him back to the relatives' room, she made him tea, to give him time to recover. He was a studious-looking man of about forty with receding brown hair and a thickening waistline. He was a schoolteacher in Oxford, he told her. The man his wife had been with was her boss, the director of an advertising company.

'He was loaded. He could afford to give her far more than I could,' Wendy's father said bitterly. Taking a crumpled handkerchief from his pocket, he blew his nose and mumbled, 'I know I shouldn't say it—but it's just as well he died too, or I-I should have wanted to kill him.'

Fiona was silent for a moment as he grappled with his feelings of despair and anger. Then she said gently, 'I'm glad you still have Wendy. It's a miracle she wasn't too badly hurt. How's she getting on?'

'They've transferred her to the children's ward for a few days. The X-ray showed a fractured cheekbone, but nothing needs to be done about it, apparently.' The father's lip trembled. 'I haven't told her yet, about her mother. I-it's a hellava situation,' he sighed.

Fiona's heart ached for him as she strove to find words of comfort. 'You'll find the right moment,' she said. 'You'll be given the strength.'

He shook his head. 'I do hope so.'

'She's going to need lots of love and support for a time. Are there any grandparents, or other relatives you can turn to?'

'Oh, yes. We're a close family; or we were, until my wife took off. It hurt everyone, as well as me,' he said ruefully. 'The ripples go far and wide.'

After he had gone Fiona had a hard job to lift her own spirits. It was at times like this that she felt at a loss. Broken bodies you could do your best to mend; broken hearts were another matter entirely. But the work of the hospital still had to go on, and the continuing demands of the general public gradually dimmed the memories of past tragedies.

There was only one permanent casualty among the staff of A and E. Aileen had been off sick ever since, and there was some doubt as to whether she would be returning.

'I do know she was very distressed,' Fiona told Molly

when the staff met up for coffee during a temporary lull the following Monday afternoon.

'So were we all,' someone else put in.

'We-ell, it affects everyone in different ways,' the sister commented peaceably. 'We all have to find the means of coping. I'll go and see her.' She began to talk about Christmas and days off, still with the smooth running of the department in mind, although she wouldn't be there. 'No annual leave for that period,' she declared, 'then everyone will get to have one of the holidays. The book's on my desk. Fill in which day you'd prefer.'

Fiona settled on having New Year's Day. She had already arranged her off-duty before Christmas to cover the weekend of her brother's wedding. Her mother and stepfather would be over from Brussels for the occasion, so they would be having some family celebrations then.

Thinking ahead brought Rory once more to mind. Not that he was ever far from her thoughts these days, and she cherished the rare moments of his company. There had been no opportunities at all for personal dealings since he'd telephoned her on the night of the major incident. He had been exceptionally busy in the operating theatre as well as being on call to the department. It had thrilled her immensely when he actually found the time to seek her out at the hospital the previous Friday evening.

'Life has been so hectic these past few days,' he had said, 'I've hardly set eyes on you. I'm off to Edinburgh now, to visit my mother. Perhaps when I get back we can have a meal together?'

His quizzical smile had made her feel breathless. Was it wishful thinking, or was there a subtle change in his manner towards her? There was certainly *something* about his unwavering gaze which suggested he liked her company. Best not to appear too eager, she had reminded herself. Hard though it was, she had answered with what she hoped was cheerful nonchalance.

'We'll have to see what we can fit in. The pace will be hotting up between now and Christmas. There's a full social calendar ahead.'

'Oh, I see.' His eyes had gleamed roguishly. 'Can I trust you to behave yourself while I'm not around?'

'Don't I always?' she'd retorted.

'Debatable.' He had left her with that bedevilling grin which completely blew her mind.

Now, filling in her off-duty for New Year's Day, she found herself wondering what Rory's plans would be for the Scottish festival. He was back from Edinburgh, she knew, although she hadn't yet seen him.

It was true what she had pointed out about the pace of things hotting up before Christmas. They were now well into November, at the end of which Molly Bland would be leaving. There was to be a farewell party for her in the social centre. A collection had already been made among the staff, which had raised enough money to buy her the tea-maker she had wanted.

The weekend following that there would be the annual Christmas Fayre, the proceeds of which would provide extras for the patients. A and E were to run a cake and handicraft stall, and, trouper that she was, Molly had already made and iced a Christmas cake to be raffled. Her cakes had become legendary at the hospital, with beautiful sugar flowers which she made and coloured herself.

'Oh, Molly, I don't know why you have to leave,' Fiona wailed. 'What are we going to do without you?'

The older woman laughed. 'You'll manage. To tell you the truth, I hate the thought of leaving, but it's no good standing still, is it? Everyone needs a new challenge from time to time.' She handed the CD keys to Fiona. 'Well, time I was off. There's that asthmatic lady—Mrs White—still in cubicle one, remember. Shirley was monitoring her. If her peak-flow has improved I should think she could go home shortly. 'Bye now. Hope you have a quiet evening.'

Molly departed, and Fiona went to check on the asthmatic patient, a middle-aged woman who had been brought in from work by one of her colleagues after a severe attack at lunchtime.

'She's feeling much better after the nebuliser treatment, aren't you, Mrs White?' Shirley said cheerfully. 'Her peak-flow reading is almost normal now.'

'And I really would like to go home, please,' Mrs White put in. 'My kids'll be wondering where I am.'

'All right,' Fiona smiled. 'I'll get the doctor to have a last look at you. What about transport home if he says you can go?'

It was agreed they would call her a taxi, to save waiting around for ambulance cover.

With the remaining few patients all receiving attention, Fiona went back to the desk to update her records. Absorbed in her work, she suddenly started, on finding Rory standing beside her.

Impressive as always, his dark grey suit sitting easily on his athletic frame, he broke through her concentration.

'Good afternoon, Effie. Busy?'

'Hello!' It was impossible to keep the pleasure out of her voice. 'No, it's been a fairly quiet afternoon,' she said. 'Did you have a good weekend?'

He perched on a corner of the desk, bringing his eyes level with hers. 'Yes, of sorts.'

'I expect your mother was pleased to see you.'

'Mmm.' He smiled, and paused before adding, 'I also saw McPhail, and I've arranged to buy the flat from him.'

'You have?' Fiona's eyes widened with interest. 'Well, it is a nice place—at least, it could be. It's got potential.'

'You mean it needs a woman's touch,' he suggested.

'Yes, if you like,' she agreed mildly.

'Come and give me the benefit of your advice, then. How about tonight?'

She shook her head. 'I'm working till nine-thirty.'

'So what? You're a night bird, aren't you?' he challenged, with what she recognised was a subtle reference to their two a.m. encounter. 'Find your way to Caversham and I'll have a meal waiting for you.'

Before she could react the peace of the afternoon was broken by a childish wailing of startling proportions. Desperately injured or ill patients were usually subdued and made little fuss. All the same, the hullabaloo was somewhat alarming.

'Whatever's that about?' Fiona jumped up and hurried to investigate.

In the waiting-room she found a distraught young couple trying to pacify a chubby little boy who appeared totally out of control, red in the face with screaming.

'What's the problem?' Fiona asked.

'I'm terribly sorry he's kicking up such a fuss, Nurse,' the flustered father apologised. 'He stuck his finger into the hole of his car seatbelt buckle, you see, and we can't get it off. Oh, do shut up, Mark, and show the lady.' He grasped the youngster's wrist in a effort to hold it forward for inspection.

Stooping to the child's level, Fiona was just able to catch a glimpse of the problem before he wriggled away again, squealing hysterically with fright and pain. Gripped tightly within the eyelet hole of the seatbelt fastening, his small forefinger was distended and purple.

'We've tried grease, and soap,' his despairing mother put in, near to tears herself.

'And we're supposed to be going on holiday tonight— flying to the Canaries,' his father said.

Fiona stood up and looked around, aware that both Rory and Adrian had come to see what was wrong. 'Did you see his finger?' she asked.

Rory nodded, looking thoughtful. 'Well, he'll not be flying anywhere with that attached.' He glanced at Adrian. 'That'll be hardened steel. A job for the fire brigade, I should think.' He scratched his cheek reflectively. 'And we'd better put him to sleep first, or it'll be impossible.'

Adrian nodded. 'I'll call the anaesthetist.'

Fiona herself went off to contact the fire brigade, leaving Rory explaining to the parents that he would need their signature for the general anaesthetic.

'It'll be just sufficient to keep him quiet for as long as it takes,' he said.

The anaesthetist arrived and was briefed as to what was required. He sized up the small patient, who redoubled his howling at the sight of another white coat. 'Just bring him through when you're ready to start,' Dr Bridge murmured, and he went to the emergency theatre to make ready his gases and a suitable face mask.

Meanwhile, Fiona produced a bag of ice to help cool down the painful little hand, and she stayed talking tranquilly to the parents as the mother cuddled the child on her knee, endeavouring to keep the ice-pack in place.

Within a short time three fire officers strode into the

department, clad in their heavy uniforms and armed with their tool-kit.

Rory glanced at Adrian. 'Right. There'll be no reasoning with this young man. It'll be a fight to get him on to the table. Your muscle or mine?'

Adrian grinned. 'Shall I let you handle it? You're bigger than me.'

'This way, laddie!' Before the toddler knew what was happening he was whisked up into a pair of strong arms and carried, protesting loudly, into the theatre. 'It'll soon be over, Mark,' the big Scot reassured him, restraining the child while the anaesthetist gradually introduced the face mask. 'Breathe away—that's right.'

Fiona couldn't help but admire Rory's firm handling of the emotional youngster. His air of command sent a delicious *frisson* over her skin. Within a few minutes the boy's struggles ceased and he was settled gently on to the table.

'OK, chaps,' said Dr Bridge, after slipping in an airway and positioning the mask firmly in place. 'I can keep him like this, no problem, for a fair bit.'

Rory examined the abused finger, then stood back while one of the firemen got to work with a hacksaw and helpful suggestions from his mates. Both sides of the bracket needed to be cut through before the finger could be released. It took some time, but at last it was accomplished, and without any surface damage to the small, turgid digit.

There were congratulations and smiles all round now that the danger was over. An on-the-spot X-ray confirmed that there was no damage beneath the skin, and Fiona provided another ice-pack to help the swelling subside.

By now it was six-thirty. 'Will you still be in time to

catch your plane?' Fiona asked when the parents were able to collect their now docile toddler.

'We should just about make it, I think,' his father said. 'And thanks so much, everyone. We're sorry to have given so much trouble.'

When everyone had dispersed after some good-natured ribaldry, Fiona tidied up the theatre and went back to the office, where she was presently joined again by Rory.

'Where did we get to before that pantomime began?' he asked with a wry grin. 'Oh, yes. You were going to find your way to Caversham after you finish here tonight.'

Her mouth fell open in protest. 'I didn't agree to anything of the kind.'

'Of course you did,' he retorted cheerfully. 'I've got a freezer full of food which the housekeeper stocked up for me. What would you like? Tandoori chicken, lasagne, plain sausage and bacon?'

She breathed in deeply and let out a long sigh. In Hampstead Rory had sought to make it plain that romance between them was not on. She was not going to win him over by obediently falling in with his every whim. More sensible not to make herself too available, she had reasoned, and for her own sanity it would be best not to weaken. The trouble was, being sensible where Rory was concerned wasn't easy.

The emergency telephone rang as she hesitated. She waved him away, saying, 'Oh, anything you like. You'd better push off before you get caught up in something else.'

'See you later, then.' Obviously pleased with himself, he went on his way.

*  *  *

The evening passed quickly with the arrival of a middle-aged man with severe chest pains who needed to be admitted to Coronary Care, but had to be kept in the department until a bed could be found. There were also a number of minor stitching and plastering jobs, and a twenty-year-old girl who had overdosed after breaking up with her boyfriend.

Adrian had gone off duty at eight o'clock, his place being taken by Dr Gale, the night locum. Dr Gale was an amiable, rotund sort of man, freelancing between hospital jobs, and it was he who helped Fiona deal with the attempted suicide.

Fiona hadn't come across Dr Gale before. She was agreeably impressed when, after they had washed out the patient, he did a great job in gaining the girl's confidence, talking to her in a kindly fashion.

They arranged for her to be warded for psychiatric help, and afterwards Dr Gale stayed chatting with Fiona, reflecting on cause and effect.

'Human relationships!' he sighed, with a sorry shake of his head. 'Half the sickness in this world is caused by love, or the lack of it.' He gave her a sideways glance. 'Have you broken any hearts lately, Miss Rogers?'

She half smiled. 'None that I know of. How about you?'

A dimple flashed in his smooth cheek. 'There's only one love in my life. Her name's *Athena*—my boat. She's more to my liking than half a dozen women.'

Fiona laughed out loud. 'Dear me! If I hadn't seen you in action with that poor kid just now, you'd have me believing you don't like people.'

'I can trot out a few apt homilies when occasion demands.' His small brown eyes twinkle. 'I'm selective—but should you ever fancy joining my crew, we could do with an extra hand in the galley.'

She laughed again. 'A woman's place is in the kitchen—even afloat? Thanks, but life on the ocean wave isn't exactly my idea of paradise.'

'Ah, well, we all have to find our own route to that particular place. And life is a series of compromises, isn't it?'

She glanced at her watch, suddenly reminded of her date with Rory and heartily wishing she had been firm about refusing to join him. 'It's time I was gone,' she told Dr Gale. 'I've just remembered, I've got a compromise to meet. Goodnight.'

Driving the short distance to the block of luxury flats by the river, Fiona smiled over her exchange with the locum. It had been one of those throwaway dialogues, of no real significance in itself. But it had started her thinking.

What was she *doing*, for goodness' sake, wasting good emotions on someone who didn't want her? Rory had said plainly enough that she couldn't have *his* heart, and he had meant it, even if it was said in a joking manner. She must stop being an idiot and wake up to reality. And there were other men in the world. Dr Gale, for instance, hadn't found her unattractive, it was obvious.

Letting herself be talked into this tête-à-tête tonight was a mistake, definitely. She would have to use it as an opportunity to establish that friendship was all she had in mind.

Her tension mounted as she parked her car, spoke into the entry-phone and took the silver lift to Rory's apartment. Making resolutions was one thing, but it didn't stop her stomach churning and her heart racing as she walked along the beige-carpeted corridor. Without work as a diversion, it wasn't going to be easy to put on a show of indifference.

He had left his door slightly ajar. She rang the bell, called 'Hello!' and went into the small entrance hall. Sounds of voices and music filtered through from the living-room as Rory appeared to welcome her.

'At last!' he said with a wide smile. 'We're all tightening our belts waiting for you.'

Her eyebrows rose in surprise as he helped her out of her duffel coat. 'Who else is here?' she asked.

'Adrian and Anna. I decided it would be no more trouble catering for four than for two. And I owed Anna some hospitality anyway.'

It crossed Fiona's mind that he also, on second thoughts, had decided against a twosome. She was vaguely disappointed because she had been determined to test her will-power, and cheered because she wouldn't now have to.

'Hi, folks!' she breezed, going in to meet the others, who were enjoying pre-dinner drinks. 'Sorry about my working togs,' she added, admiring Anna's smart black trousers and long stylish sweater. 'He didn't ask me till tonight, so I didn't have time to go home and change.'

'As I said, this was all very spur-of-the-moment,' Rory put in smoothly. 'Don't worry! It's what's inside the dress that counts.'

His easy charm, ever ready with the melting rejoinder, made her more than relieved he had invited the others, or all her good resolutions might have gone to the wall. To depersonalise matters she sniffed the air appreciatively. 'Mmm! Something smells good.'

Anna grinned at her. She was looking extremely attractive with her shoulder-length red hair loose and bouncy. 'He's been doing mysterious things in the kitchen,' she said. 'I offered to help, but he turned me down.'

The oval walnut dining table was already set with place mats and cutlery, a wine glass and a white paper napkin at each place.

'Sit yourselves down, girls,' said Rory, 'and Adrian, you can pour the wine for me while I bring in the starters.'

To begin with there was smoked salmon on a bed of crisp greenery. This was followed by a creamy chicken dish with broccoli, and chunks of French bread, and for dessert a refreshing lemon sorbet. It was an unhurried meal, enlivened with a great deal of good humoured small talk. Rory did all the serving himself and refused help with clearing up afterwards.

'I'll do it when you've gone,' he said. 'Sit down and talk among yourselves while I make coffee. Won't be a moment.'

Fiona sat back in one of the deep leather armchairs and glanced about her. 'I'd an idea this was supposed to be a how-to-improve-my-flat session. Has he been picking your brains, Anna?'

'No. Before you arrived we'd been talking about the difference between last Monday and this. You know— the carry-on you had today with that little boy and his trapped finger.'

'Oh, that.' Fiona smiled, remembering. 'I wonder if they managed to catch their plane?'

'We did our best for them, anyway,' said Adrian. 'We couldn't have worked any faster.'

Their host came in with the coffee-pot and mugs on a tray, and set them on a low table. 'Will you pour for me, Anna?' He sat opposite Fiona. 'Come on now, girls, thinking caps on,' he pronounced cheerfully. 'What does this place need to make it more like home?'

'A wife?' Adrian suggested drily.

'Pipe down, laddie,' Rory joked. 'I want *good* advice. That could be a recipe for disaster.'

Fiona rolled her eyes. 'Oh, no, not *another* professed misogynist. I just left one of those behind at the hospital.'

'Who was that?' Rory asked.

'Just one of the locums.' Fiona settled herself more comfortably. 'There's nothing wrong with these chairs. They're great—except you could use a few nice cushions.'

Anna looked at the ceiling-to-floor curtains. They were of sea-green satinised material with a modern leafy-brown design which toned in well against the mottled brownish carpet. 'The curtains are fine. Too good to discard,' she added with true Scottish thrift. 'You could do with a nice picture on one of the walls, though.'

'And how about a plant of some kind—a weeping fig, or a monstera, over there?' Fiona indicated.

Rory chuckled. 'I haven't got time to pander to the needs of house plants. If you want to turn the place into Kew Gardens you'll have to promise to come in and do the watering.'

Time drifted pleasurably by with background music from Rory's latest CD acquisition, the soundtrack from the Lloyd Webber musical Cats. Anna was something of a chatterbox, although not in a boring way, and it amused Fiona to see the quiet admiration in Adrian's eyes. She wondered whether Rory had invited Anna for himself, or if he were consciously playing Cupid. At least while Anna talked Fiona could enjoy Rory's company without attention being drawn to herself.

It was after midnight when Anna decided it was time

to be leaving. She had obviously come with Adrian who asked if Fiona needed a lift.

'No, thanks. I've got my own car downstairs,' she returned.

'Well, in that case we'll push off, shall we, Adrian?' Anna said. 'Thanks for a lovely evening, Rory.'

Their goodbyes said, they were gone before Fiona had time to collect her wits. 'There go two happy people,' she said as Rory closed the door behind them. 'Did you—er—realise that Adrian was keen on Anna?'

'Yes, I had sussed that one out.' He smiled whimsically. 'I thought a little shove in the right direction might not come amiss.'

Fiona patted a pretend yawn, battling against her rising tension, striving to maintain her serenity for just another few minutes. 'I ought to be going, too,' she said lightly, 'unless you'd like some help with the chores?'

'Thanks, but it's all right. I'll get my lady to do it for me tomorrow—she's very obliging. Shall we have another coffee together?'

His slow, heart-stopping smile made her breath come quickly. She shook her head. 'I've enjoyed the evening very much, but I do have to be up early in the morning.'

He put a hand on her shoulder, a questioning look in his eyes. 'Is that the real reason? It's not that you're afraid to be alone with me, is it?'

She managed a laugh, although her heart was thundering in her chest. 'Good heavens, no! I didn't imagine you were about to try it on with your best friend's little sister.'

His mouth screwed into a roguish grin. 'I *could* be tempted, Effie. I'm very fond of you. I didn't realise how much—until I wondered whether you'd been caught up in that motorway nightmare. The sight of a car similar to yours, crushed to a pancake. . .' He suddenly pulled her into his arms in a fierce embrace. 'Oh, God! When I saw you meeting the ambulance it was like waking from a bad dream.'

Although her body throbbed with longing at his show of affection, Fiona steeled herself to resist. She *wouldn't* succumb to his petting just when the fancy took him, because he wasn't saying that he loved her, was he? He was only admitting to a certain amount of friendly regard.

She pulled away from his loving arms, feeling fighting mad. 'Rory, back in Hampstead you were warning *me* not to flirt with *you*. So what's this all about?'

He thrust his hands into his pockets and stood back with an apologetic half-smile. 'I wish I knew. I'm just a normal male, Effie. I'm not totally proof against your feminine charms.'

Anger helped her to resist the clamour of her body wanting his. If he had discovered that he loved her yet wasn't prepared to admit it, then she wasn't going to make it easy for him by falling into his arms at the first approach. He was going to have to do the thing properly, not just make a fuss of her when it suited him. It had to be all or nothing.

'That's all the more reason for me to be leaving, then,' she declared. 'Goodnight!' and she went to grab her duffel coat from where it was hanging, biting her lips to hold back the tears. She would *not* let him see how much he could hurt her.

He followed her into the hall, his expression disgruntled. 'I'd better come with you, to make sure you arrive. It's a murky night.'

'Don't be ridiculous,' she returned coolly. 'I've been

driving myself around for yonks. I managed perfectly well before you came on the scene.'

'All the same, it's my fault you're out at this hour, so I shall see you to your door, as I should do if I'd been able to collect you properly in the first place. I'll follow on behind you in my car. Right?'

She shrugged and made a careless gesture. 'Please yourself, Mr Perfect. I can't stop you.'

They went down together in the lift, both silent, he with his hands anchored in his trouser pockets, she looking anywhere but at his indomitable face. His weak moment appeared to have passed and he now seemed totally in control. She, on the other hand, felt like a jelly in danger of collapse.

It was an enormous relief when they were out on the forecourt with the night breeze to cool her hot cheeks. Chin in the air, she began marching towards her Fiesta.

'Wait there,' Rory ordered. 'I have to get my car out of the garage.'

Wait for him? No chance! Fiona fastened her seatbelt, switched on the engine, backed, and was through the entrance gates and shooting along the road before Rory had pushed up his garage door.

He caught up with her at the second lot of traffic lights and stayed behind her all the way. She was trembling as she drove into her own parking bay at Sycamore Grange and walked back to the house.

Rory was standing there waiting for her, a veritable tower of contained umbrage. 'You were told to wait for me,' he said severely.

'And I said you needn't bother to come.' Turning away, she singled out her door-key from the bunch.

He grabbed her arm, demanding, 'What's got into you? Why the devil are you being like this?'

'I'm not being like anything. I'm very tired, and I want to go to bed, *if* you don't mind,' she retorted.

'God give me strength!' he despaired. 'Bangladesh was a piece of cake compared to dealing with you.'

She stood there mutely, unbending as his eyes searched her stony face. So he bent and kissed her full on the lips, and it took every ounce of her will-power to remain impassive.

He studied her again, holding her at arm's length. 'You know,' he murmured, 'there's a splendid old adage which says, "Never let the sun go down upon your wrath." *I* don't even know why we're quarrelling. I've kissed you to make up. Now you kiss me.'

Fiona couldn't help a faint smile at his martyred expression. 'You're lucky I have a forgiving nature,' she said, and offered her lips to his, unable to resist his persuasion.

It might have started as a brief kiss of forgiveness, but that was not the way it finished.

'Friends again?' Rory asked.

'Yes.' She looked up into his soul-searching eyes. 'Even friends fall out sometimes.'

'True!' He laughed softly, and quite naturally his arms went around her as he kissed her again. Only this time the pressure of his mouth on hers was more prolonged, and she couldn't help but respond.

The result was electrifying, sending her senses wild. His embrace tightened. She couldn't believe—didn't want to believe—that this meant nothing to him beyond a mild flirtation.

All too soon he let her go. 'Oh, dear! I mustn't start again. Go to bed, lass.' And with a whispered, 'Goodnight!' he left her.

Afterwards it was difficult to decide whether her weakening had been a mistake. It must surely be no secret now how she felt about him. If she got hurt she would have only herself to blame.

# CHAPTER TEN

THE days that followed had Fiona in a curious kind of limbo. At the back of her mind was a certain conviction that, despite what he had said to the contrary, Rory's feelings for her went deeper than friendship, if only he would admit it. As for herself, her need for him had become a constant, monstrous ache. Undeniably, here was the man she hungered to spend the rest of her life with. But she could hardly blatantly come out and tell him so. She had to preserve at least a little dignity. After all, she *might* have got it wrong. Supposing she didn't stir any fires for him?

The more she wrestled with the problem the more impossible it seemed. There was really nothing she could do except stand back, be herself and let things take their natural course.

Having come to that conclusion did seem to bring her a kind of acceptance. If Rory was not for her, then she would just have to bear it and thank her stars that at least she had a satisfying career to engage in. Rory had commandeered her heart whether he'd intended to or not. She wanted no one else.

It had been a busy week, the A and E department crowded out with the fractures, sprains and chest complaints accompanying wintry weather. On the Friday morning of Molly Bland's last day, trees and hedgerows were rimed with white frost and there was ice on the puddles as Fiona drove in to work.

At the Memorial Hospital the night staff had been

kept busy, it wasn't surprising to hear. Giving his handover report to the day shift, the charge nurse told them that Rory Kinross was already in Theatre dealing with an RTA which had happened earlier. Another severely injured young man had just been admitted to Resus, the victim of a head-on car collision.

'He's Tim Forest, twenty years old,' the charge nurse detailed. 'Multiple injuries—compound fractures tib and fib, possibly femur, and facial lacerations. We've started an IVI of Haemaccel and the doctor's taken blood. We've ordered four units of cross-matched.'

Molly directed Fiona and Rosemary to go and take over the casualty from the night nurses. 'I'll get Damien to come along as soon as he arrives,' she said.

The night casualty officer was the same Dr Gale whom Fiona had met previously. He gave her a tired but welcome smile of recognition.

'Good morning! *Not* such a good one for our friend here, I'm afraid.' He glanced kindly at the rugged young man on the stretcher while carefully checking to find pulses in his feet. 'Mmm, that seems OK. We've been doing fifteen-minute observations. I should keep that up until someone else sees him, girls.' He left them, saying he wanted a word with the incoming doctor.

Fiona took over the charts from the two night nurses, who had cut off the patient's clothes and got him into an examination gown.

'The ambulance crew didn't think he was KO'd,' the staff nurse told her. 'He's had 60 mgs of codeine phos for the pain. He's been very brave.' She leaned over to say goodbye to her patient. 'Cheerio, Tim. The day staff will look after you now. Keep smiling.'

The youth lifted his free hand in a feeble salute. 'Thanks for everything,' he murmured.

Introducing herself and Rosemary, Fiona said gently, 'Let's clean you up a bit while we're waiting for the doctor. Your face may not be as bad as it looks.'

Uncovering a dressings trolley, she put on gloves and carefully swabbed away the dried blood and dirt from his cheeks, nose and chin, revealing a couple of ugly gashes which would need stitching.

Damien arrived, pulling a long face at Fiona in the light of his talk with Dr Gale. He assumed a more confident expression for the patient, pushing back his floppy fair hair as he bent over the youth.

'Hello, old son. I'm Dr Crewe,' he announced. 'How are you feeling?'

Although obviously still in pain, the patient was doing his best to be stoical. 'Battered, if not fried,' he returned with an attempt at levity.

They all smiled, and Fiona had to admit that Damien had improved a lot in his handling of patients. He was turning into a caring casualty officer. Now, after making his own careful examination, he was thoughtful for a moment.

'Kinross and Imran are tied up for now,' he pondered. 'I suppose the best we can do is get X-rays done. Better have the portable along here, hadn't we? And do something about those cuts on his face, Fiona. I can leave you to suture those, can't I?' he enquired with a touch of his old self-importance.

Fiona nodded in compliance, while Rosemary seethed with indignation after the doctor had left them.

'She's done more stitching than he's had hot dinners,' she assured the patient. 'Don't worry, Tim.'

'I won't, if you promise to keep holding my hand,' he cracked.

The X-raying session finished, Fiona scrubbed up and

put on fresh sterile gloves before injecting a local anaesthetic and putting in the necessary sutures. She had just
finished her task when a firm hand squeezed her
shoulder, and glancing up, she found Rory there with
Damien, and her pulse put on its usual frisk.

The consultant was still in his theatre garb. He gave
her a passing smile as he approached the injured boy.
'Hello! Tim isn't it? I'm Kinross, orthopaedic surgeon.
Now, let me see what I can do for you.'

After a rapid clinical assessment, he studied the X-
rays, slotting them one after the other into the lighted
viewing box and deciding upon surgery as soon as the
theatre could be made ready. 'Get the leg immobilised
in a Thomas's splint. IV pethidine first,' he advised
Damien. 'Pain is debilitating, so we don't want to subject
him to more than he already has. And start the blood as
soon as it comes.' In a teasing aside to Fiona, he
murmured, 'You're aware of the dangers of blood loss in
injury to the femur, aren't you?'

'Oh, yes,' she murmured back. 'It's indelibly printed
on my memory.'

Having been informed that the youth's mother had
arrived and was in the relatives' room, the consultant
left to talk to her. Meanwhile the nurses did what they
had to do for their patient, inevitably hurting him a little
now and then, but praising him for his courage.

He had gone to Theatre by the time the two nurses
went for their lunch, where Fiona was a captive audience
while Rosemary daydreamed about the brave and handsome Tim.

'Isn't he terrific?' Rosemary sighed. 'That's the kind
of guy I could go for in a big way. Wish I was going to
be nursing him on the ward. Do you think he'd remember me if I went to see him?'

Fiona grinned. 'Highly likely, I'd say. Anyway, you're sure to see him around later. He'll be coming up to the fracture clinic once he gets out of here.'

On returning from lunch Fiona was surprised to receive a summons to go and see the senior nursing officer. 'What's it about?' she asked, mystified, when Molly passed on the message.

'You'll see—nothing wrong,' the sister said. 'I should sponge that smear of blood off your uniform before you go.'

Fiona shot along to the staff-room, removed the offending bloodstain from the skirt of her white uniform, tidied her hair and made her way back to the SNO's quarters.

'You wanted to see me, Mrs Newsome?' she said brightly, after knocking and being told to enter.

'Nurse Rogers—yes. Come and sit down.' The SNO indicated a chair, took off her reading glasses and gave Fiona a generally appraising glance. 'You applied for Sister Bland's post some weeks ago,' she began. 'As I said at the time, we were unable to consider you then, for the reason I explained.' She rested her elbows on the desk and steepled her fingers while approving the alert, confident manner of the girl opposite. 'Are you still interested in taking a sister's post here?' she asked.

Her eyebrows lifting in surprise, Fiona swallowed. 'Well, yes, of course. But I would really only qualify for that in A and E,' she felt constrained to point out. 'It's the work I know best. I'm rather out of touch with ward procedures.'

Mrs Newsome nodded. 'I understand that, but it's in Casualty that another vacancy has come about.' She went on to explain. 'At a recent meeting it was agreed that the demands of our A and E Department, with our proximity to the motorway, warranted an increase in senior staff. It was decided to create a new junior sister's post, and we're offering it to you if you'd like it.'

Fiona's cheeks flushed with pleasure. 'Oh, I certainly would!' she said, after getting her breath back. 'Gosh! That's wonderful. Thank you very much.'

The SNO beamed. 'It's a joy to be the bringer of good news sometimes. I'm sure you'll like working with Sister North. By the way, she won't be starting with you for another two weeks yet. She's taking some overdue holiday first. But by all accounts you've shown yourself quite capable of coping.'

'Fingers crossed we don't get another major incident,' Fiona returned with a happy laugh. 'Although we've got a great team of nurses on at the moment. Since that last pile-up we've all grown closer somehow.'

The older woman nodded. 'Yes, that often happens when you're involved in something big. Well, we'll take it that's settled. Your new contract will start from the beginning of December. Go along to the sewing room and get yourself measured for your blue uniforms.' She put a hand out to shake Fiona's. 'Congratulations, Sister Rogers. I've watched your progress here. I know you'll make a success of this.'

Going back to A and E after visiting the sewing-room, Fiona walked on air. For all her initial hesitance about moving up a grade, it was thrilling to know that other people had confidence in her. Besides which, it might even improve her standing with Rory.

She almost cannoned into Damien as he came from one of the cubicles armed with some blood samples.

'Watch where you're going, girl,' he drawled. 'What are you looking so chuffed about?'

She could even have kissed Damien on his smooth,

supercilious cheek. 'You treat me with respect now, Doctor,' she said, pushing a finger into his white-coated ribs. 'It's Sister Rogers now, or it will be in a few days' time.'

'Ho, ho! No wonder you're fizzing. I'll take you out for a celebratory drink tonight, if you like.'

'Well, that's very sweet of you, Damien,' she said, willing to love the whole world, 'but it's Molly's leaving party at the social centre, remember? Maybe I'll see you over there.'

The news filtered throughout the department, and everyone was pleased for her.

Bea said, 'About time too. You've been acting for long enough without pay.'

Even Aileen, who had come back to work that week, wished her joy of it, although in a disgruntled fashion. Aileen had given in her notice in favour of a job in a private hospital, which would be more to her liking than the hectic pace of A and E, she had decided. 'But I wouldn't have stood a chance here, with you being so thick with Rory Kinross,' she had to add.

'Kinross?' Fiona echoed, frowning. 'I don't think he had anything to do with it. Mrs Newsome said they'd had this in mind for some time.'

'Well, if you believe that, you'll believe anything,' Aileen scoffed.

It worried Fiona more than a little. She hoped Aileen was wrong. She certainly didn't want to be obligated to Rory for her promotion.

Later that afternoon the consultant was once more in the department to see a casualty. Determined to stay out of his way, Fiona left Bea to deal with his needs. However, deep in thought as she made for the staff-room en route for home, the deep timbre of his voice broke through to her as their paths crossed.

'Weighty matters on your mind?' he joked. 'Try me. I fix other things besides broken bones.'

She started, and smiled. 'Oh, I thought you'd gone,' she said.

Taking in her uncertain expression, he asked, 'Did you want me for something?'

Instinctively she avoided the subject of her promotion, feeling he might bring it up himself if he had been involved. 'No, not specially.' She fabricated an excuse for her remark. 'I was just wondering how that nice boy Tim got on. Did you manage to fix him up OK?'

'Yes. We screwed him together, and nature will do the rest in time. Hopefully.'

'I'm glad of that. One of the junior nurses will be thrilled to know he's going to be all right.'

'Made a conquest, did he?' Rory gave a crooked grin. 'It never stops, does it?'

'What's that?' Fiona queried, her mind more on the delicious outline of his lips than what he was saying.

'The pull of the sexes. That certain something which catches people off guard, and they don't know what's hit them.'

'Oh, that old thing!' By a sheer act of will she met his teasing blue eyes levelly. 'You probably know far more about it than I do—at your *superior* age,' she mocked.

'Actually, my defences have been taking quite a battering of late,' he admitted, and, although there was humour in his quiet voice, his unwavering gaze set her blood surging.

But somewhere between last Monday and now Fiona had struggled through to firm ground. Outwardly she appeared cool, although inwardly she was a shambles trying to decide how to react to his cue. It was no good him dropping hints only to back off when it came to the crunch, she mused. She would *not* make the running. She would not bare her heart for him, unless he was prepared to do the same.

She smiled equably. 'There's an easy answer to that, surely, if it bothers you.'

'Is there? Tell me.'

'Drop your defences?' she suggested sweetly.

Rory sighed. 'If only it were that simple.'

'Why can't it be?'

He declined to answer. Just stood there looking at her with his dark head on one side, an impenetrable expression on his suddenly serious face.

Her impulse was to reach up and kiss him, long and lovingly. Out of the question, of course, especially seeing where they were. 'I give up!' she declared with a flamboyant gesture. 'Find your own solution.' With that she went on her way, hoping against hope that she was playing this right.

Back at her flat she switched on the radio and made herself some toast and coffee before getting ready for Molly's party, making a great effort to push Rory out of her mind. But a programme of love songs only made matters worse, accentuating her longings for the unattainable. She switched off the music and was about to take a shower when her telephone rang.

'Craig—hello!' she exclaimed as her ex-boyfriend's voice jolted her back to the past. It dawned on her a little guiltily that not once had she thought about Craig since they'd parted a fortnight ago—proof positive that she'd made the right decision there.

'How are you?' she asked brightly.

'OK, except I'm getting bored with this British weather. How's it with you?'

'Fine. We've been madly busy at work, so there's not been much time for socialising, I'm afraid.' She wondered if he thought she should have been in touch before.

'Yes, I read about your hospital having to deal with that shambles on the motorway. Was it a bad experience?'

'Pretty grim, although we coped at the time. It's afterwards you wonder how you did. Actually I think it did me a service in a way.' She told him about her unexpected promotion to junior sister.

'Good for you! So no chance you'll give any more thought to working in the States, then?' he asked.

'No, Craig, I'm sorry. There wasn't even before the sister's job came up.'

'So that's it, then.' He sounded rueful. 'I'm afraid I haven't had a chance to get up to see you. I've been doing some agency work to earn a few beans. Could you get up to town before I go back, do you think?'

Fiona reminded him about her brother's wedding in two weeks' time. 'So I've had to save my off-duty for that. Maybe we could fit in something then. Otherwise, we'll write sometimes, eh?'

'Yes, I'd like us to keep doing that,' Craig said. 'My one regret about working over there is that it came between us.'

'That's life,' she said. 'You'll find someone else.' After talking for a little while longer they signed off, wishing each other well.

Relieved at having that period of her life finally over, and no hard feelings, Fiona returned to getting ready for the evening's festivities. It was important to be there on time for the presentations to Molly, and the spoken tributes. And although many of the upper hierarchy would probably disappear after a decent interval, the partying would go on for as long as people wished to stay.

Casual dress again being the order of the day, Fiona eased into her black stretch cords, which she teamed with a cream silk sleeveless top and a colourful patterned overshirt. On the spur of the moment she decided against driving herself and phoned for a taxi. Lois would be dropping in on the party when she came off duty at nine-thirty, and in all probability they would come home together.

The social centre at the hospital had already been decorated in readiness for Christmas. Fiona arrived to find the place garlanded with paper chains, tinsel and balloons, and a large artificial Christmas tree glittered with fairy lights. Molly was already there, attractively dressed in a saxe-blue silky two-piece, being dutifully looked after by Adrian and Damien, among the many well-wishers surrounding her.

After hanging up her jacket on one of the pegs, Fiona bounded over to greet Molly and admire the many gifts which had been set out on a table.

'Aren't I lucky!' The sister's round face glowed with happiness. 'Everyone's been so generous.'

'You deserve it,' Fiona declared warmly. 'We're all going to miss you like crazy.'

'We certainly are,' Damien agreed. 'Especially since we're going to have to put up with *this* wench in your place.' He threw an impudent grin in Fiona's direction.

Adrian gave her a friendly wink. 'Take no notice of that ratbag. A smashing choice, if I may say so.'

Damien put an arm around her shoulders. 'Yes, only joking, sweetheart.'

Meanwhile, Rory had quietly arrived on the scene. He said good evening, and glanced around at the laughing faces. 'What was the joke?

'Oh, they were taking the mickey, about my promotion,' Fiona told him. 'At least, Damien. . .'

'What promotion?' the consultant asked.

Molly explained. 'Fiona's been appointed to the new junior sister's post they've created for A and E. Didn't you know? I think you may have been away when they had that meeting.'

Rory stroked his chin thoughtfully. 'Well done, Fiona,' he murmured.

'Thank you. Not that I had a great deal to do with it, except to fill in that form, which you chivvied me into doing in the first place.' She paused to look at him. 'Someone even put it to me that you'd been pulling strings.'

'No, I had nothing to do with it. You should know by now, Fiona, that I believe in people pulling their own strings,' he said.

Adrian polished his glasses and said, with a modest smile, 'I'm celebrating tonight too.' They all turned to look at him, and he went on, 'I heard this evening—I got that job I applied for in Oxford. I'm to join Monro's firm as registrar in the new year.'

There were cries of delight, and shaking of hands, and hearty congratulations.

'More changes!' Fiona sighed. 'No sooner do you get used to people than they're off.'

'Never mind, you still have me,' Damien crowed. 'That must be a great comfort to you.'

She chuckled. 'Oh, it is. Terrific.' But she missed the frown that settled between Rory's brows as he listened to their good-natured banter.

Other consultants and senior administrators had by now arrived, and there followed the tributes and presentations to the well-respected sister who was moving on. Afterwards, the houseman in charge of the music set the dancing in progress, and Rory escorted Molly on to the floor.

'OK, sweetheart, let you and me show them how it's done!' Damien pulled Fiona into the action. He was an excellent dancer, and she had to admit to enjoying his agility.

'We make a perfect pair, you know,' he said pulling up by the bar when the music finished and ordering drinks for them both. 'Dancing partners, you mean,' she said, her cheeks pink, her eyes sparkling.

'Not only that.' He tweaked a wayward strand of her sunny hair. 'I like your style. You're a challenge.'

'A challenge to what?'

'My male ego, girl. The taming of the shrew and all that.'

'I'm not a shrew,' she protested. 'I aim to be lovely to everyone.'

'Just be lovely to me and forget the rest, eh?'

She shook her head and giggled. 'No way, Damien. You should go for a stunning brunette to contrast with your lion locks. The attraction of opposites, et cetera.'

He feigned a punch at her chin. 'You talk too much. What *you* need is taking to bed. How about it?'

Fiona laughed again. 'Tut, tut, Doctor. Dancing partners, yes. Sleeping partners, no.'

'Oh, well, I'll have to work on it,' he returned flippantly. 'Come on then, let's dance.'

He kept her busy until there was a lull in the proceedings with the arrival of buffet-style refreshments. She had occasional glimpses of Rory in conversation with senior management, dancing with Anna and other nurses, and once, when their eyes had met, she caught a distinct message of disapproval in her direction. Was he jealous? she wondered. Well, it was all up to him.

Excusing herself from Damien on seeing Lois arrive with other latecomers, Fiona was about to make her way over when Rory intercepted her.

'That young Romeo's been monopolising you most of the evening,' he growled. 'I haven't been able to get a look in. Do you like the guy?'

'Damien? He's harmless,' she said mildly. 'I enjoy dancing with him.'

'Oh, is that meant to reassure me? How are you getting home tonight—got your car here?'

'Actually, no. I was about to cadge a lift with Lois— unless you're offering to take me,' she added with a cheeky grin.

'That could be arranged,' he returned, smiling back. 'I have to go over to Paget to check on a patient, but I shouldn't be long. I've promised to run Molly home with her presents, whenever she's ready. Will you come along with me?'

She nodded, a little surprised at her own temerity and thrilled at his reaction. 'Yes, I'd love to.'

She continued over to join Lois, feeling ridiculously optimistic, her hopes burgeoning.

Lois had yet to hear about the events of the day, and when told of Fiona's unexpected rise in status she was truly delighted. 'Oh, that's marvellous,' she enthused. 'No wonder you're looking on top of the world. Is that what you were talking about to Rory just now?'

'Not at that moment,' Fiona confessed. 'He was arranging to take me home, after we've delivered Molly with her presents.'

Her friend's eyebrows formed a question mark, and Fiona wrinkled her nose and laughed.

Half an hour later Rory was back. Fiona had been keeping her eye on the door, and suddenly there he was—vital and handsome, inflaming her senses, making her catch her breath as usual. Moreover, he seemed in remarkably good spirits, but she thought that might possibly be because all was well on the ward. Nothing to do with her and him.

Molly had begun circulating, saying her final good-byes. Presently Adrian took it upon himself to go over to the old upright piano where he rattled a few impressive chords, building up to 'Auld Lang Syne'.

Joining in the final accolade with Damien on one side of her and Rory on the other, Fiona thrilled to the consultant's deep voice lustily swelling the sound.

Afterwards she said nostalgically, 'The end of an era. I wonder who else will have moved on by this time next year?'

Damien's arm went around her waist. 'Me, for a start. But you play your cards right, and——Oh! I forgot, you don't play cards, do you?' he mocked.

'We seem to have had this conversation before,' said Fiona, laughing and freeing herself from his hold.

Glancing from one to the other, Rory was unamused but curious. However, further repartee was drowned out in the noisy goodbyes that followed.

Having singled out her jacket from the pile of coats on the pegs, Fiona then helped with carrying Molly's packages to Rory's car.

Molly herself had a moped which she normally used to cover the fifteen-minute drive from her apartment to the hospital. It was a modern flat, on the first floor of a sprawling functional block surrounded by trim lawns.

Tonight, having travelled in greater comfort in Rory's car, she apologised for the dimly lit stone staircase that led to her front door.

'It's the only thing that spoils the place,' she said, pushing through swing doors to a carpeted landing and feeling in her pocket for her key. 'I've been really happy here. I'll be sorry to leave.'

'Do you rent it?' Rory asked.

'No, I was buying it. I shall let it furnished for the time being. I'm going into hospital accommodation in London until I find something else.'

The living-room she let them into was quite roomy and comfortably furnished on a leaf-patterned fitted carpet. 'Thanks for your help,' she said, switching on wall-lights and a table lamp. 'The chap next door did offer, but I told him I was being looked after.'

Molly was a very self-contained person, and Fiona suddenly realised she knew very little about the sister's private life. Now, setting the box she was carrying down on the table, she noticed a clarinet lying in its case on a chair. And there was a music stand with a sheet of music on it. 'Molly, do you play that?' she asked in surprise.

The sister gave a modest smile. 'Yes. I used to play at school. I only took it up again a couple of years ago. My friend next door encouraged me—he's a violinist. We both play in the local symphony orchestra.' She made a regretful face. 'That's another thing I'm going to miss.'

'It's a lovely hobby to have,' Rory enthused. 'You shouldn't give it up. You're bound to find another orchestra somewhere.'

There was a short ring at her front doorbell. 'That'll be Max, wanting to know how the party went,' Molly beamed, and opened the door to let in her musical neighbour. Introductions followed to the genial middle-aged man and there was a light-hearted exchange of pleasantries. 'Would you all like coffee?' Molly asked.

Fiona hesitated. She exchanged glances with Rory, then decided that the friends might prefer to be left together. 'I think we really ought to be going, if you don't mind,' she said. And so they kissed goodbye, wished each other well for the future and promised to keep in touch.

Traipsing back down the stone staircase, Fiona smiled to herself. 'Molly's a dark horse,' she said. 'I'd no idea she was musical, or that she had a gentleman friend.'

'Yes, there's a lot we don't know about the people we work with,' Rory observed. 'What do you do in your spare time that I don't know about? Besides causing me a fair amount of aggravation, that is.'

She wrinkled her nose at him. 'I don't seem to have a great deal of spare time. Play badminton when I can, and swim. Read, write letters.' She should have added, *and daydream about you*, but she went on to say, 'Adrian's hot stuff on the piano, isn't he? I didn't know that either.'

They had arrived at the car and he paused to unlock her door. 'And *I* couldn't follow what it was you were talking about with Damien at the end of the evening. Private joke, was it?'

'Oh, it was nothing. Just one of his fatuous remarks. He's always trying to be clever.'

'Hmm!' Rory went round to his own side of the car and started up. 'Will you come back to my place for that drink?'

'Yes, if you'd like me to,' she said.

'I would, very much. There's a lot I want to say to you, and it's too cold to sit in the car. We may as well be comfortable.'

The red BMW purred quietly along the dark roads. Fiona folded her hands in her lap and gazed out at the frostbitten countryside, her tension increasing with every mile. There could be lots of things he wanted to talk to her about, not necessarily personal, intimate ones. But there was something in the way he had looked at her which made her quiver. Dared she hope?

# CHAPTER ELEVEN

'I DID wonder,' Fiona said thoughtfully, 'whether it might be a good idea for me to rent Molly's flat. Of course, she may already have someone——'

'Aren't you happy where you are?' Rory cut in.

'Yes, but it's hospital property, and——'

'I should stay with it for the time being,' he advised. 'You're among friends, and that place did have a rather barracks-like setting. Sycamore Grange has nicer surroundings.'

The miles slipped by towards the more luxurious layout of Rory's home. 'So when are we going to see you in your new blue frock and frilly cap?' he asked, flashing her a sideways smile.

'Some time next week. I was told they'd be ready after the weekend, but I'm off on Monday and Tuesday. Anyway, I've got to buy some black duty shoes first,' Fiona chatted. 'And I need to buy some shoes to go with my bridesmaid dress. Not long now, is it?'

'No. About the wedding, Effie, I phoned your brother earlier this evening,' Rory mentioned casually.

'Did you?' She turned her eyes to his strong profile while he negotiated the roundabout ahead. 'Any special reason?'

'We needed to talk about arrangements. I understand Deborah's parents are to have relatives staying at their house, so you and she will leave from Hampstead.' Rory grinned. 'Apparently it's considered unlucky for the bride and groom to meet on the morning of the wedding.'

'Of course!' Fiona laughed. 'Even though they've lived together for the past six years. Some things may change, but never the age-old customs.'

Halting at traffic-lights, he turned towards her. 'How much time have you arranged for that weekend?'

'I've got Friday afternoon and right through to Sunday. That will give me time with Mummy and my stepfather when James and Debs have gone away. Otherwise it would fall a bit flat for them.'

'Fine. That suits me.' His enquiring eyes held hers. 'We are driving up together, aren't we?'

'I'm counting on it.'

His gaze lingered on her honeyed complexion and her engaging features, so warm and vivacious. 'What colour is your bridesmaid's dress?'

'A sort of peachy-pink. I don't suppose I shall ever wear it again,' Fiona lamented, 'and it's gorgeous.'

As he waited for the traffic-lights to change his fingers drummed on the steering-wheel. 'You'll look like a wild rose,' he said.

'Not a tame rose?'

He grinned and placed a large hand over one of hers. 'Heaven forbid! It's that independent, feisty streak in you I admire.'

Her eyes widened and she swallowed. 'Did you say— *admire*?'

'Yes, but don't let it go to your head.'

'I'm quite sure you'll see that it doesn't.'

The lights signalled green and they continued their journey. Arriving at his flat, they stood close together while the small lift carried them up to the second floor. Both were unusually silent. The tantalising nearness of Rory's virile body made Fiona ache to be in his arms, so she kept her hands in her pockets and looked anywhere but at his face.

'What, no cushions or pot plants yet?' she remarked teasingly, glancing around when they came into his living-room. 'A fat lot of good it was asking for our opinions only to ignore them.'

Rory controlled a smile. 'I haven't, not entirely. I came to the conclusion that Adrian's idea was the best. Only that wasn't instantly available.'

'What was that?' she asked, although she thought she remembered.

'That what I really needed was a wife. Going to take off your jacket?' He proceeded to unbutton it for her, and, because they were so close, it seemed perfectly natural that he should kiss her afterwards, in a playful sort of way. He then threw off his own jacket and loosened his tie. 'Have a seat. I'll get the coffee going.'

Unwilling to lose a precious moment of his company, she followed him as he made towards the kitchen. Leaning against the edge of the pine table, she watched him busy with cafetière and coffee grounds, savouring the ripple of his muscles beneath his blue-striped shirt.

'Is James having a stag night?' she asked.

'Yes, next week. But I shan't manage to be there for that.' He turned to look at her while waiting for the kettle to boil. 'James and I also talked about you. . .' he began.

'Me?' She frowned, until something occurred to her. 'Oh, you mean about the sister's job?'

'No, I didn't mention that. There was something important that I needed to check out with him.' At that point his telephone rang. He grabbed it off the wall impatiently. 'Kinross here.'

There followed a peremptory exchange, concluding

with a sigh of resignation as Rory said, 'OK, I'll be there in about fifteen minutes.' Replacing the receiver, he wiped a hand over his face and groaned, 'Well timed, Damien!'

'What's up?' Fiona asked.

'Sorry, Effie,' he returned, steering her back towards the living-room. 'Coats on again, and forget the coffee. Your friend Damien has had a fall, busted his elbow and dislocated his shoulder. My registrar's away, so I've got to go and sort the fellow out.'

Back they went along the corridor to the lift. 'Poor Damien,' Fiona said with a half-laugh. 'Be gentle with him, won't you?'

'I'm not a sadist, my love,' he growled. This time in the lift he caught her in a bear-hug. 'There was such a lot I wanted to say to you tonight,' he murmured huskily. 'Ah, well, this is what you have to put up with if you get involved with doctors.'

'Will it be a long job?' she asked.

'Maybe tricky. Elbows can be difficult.'

'I know—must be painful too. It's bad enough just knocking your funnybone.'

They were back in the car now and speeding towards Sycamore Grange, which was en route to the hospital.

'We'll continue our rendezvous at the first opportunity,' Rory promised. 'And at a more reasonable hour. Would you like to have dinner at Sonning again?'

Fiona chewed her thumbnail for a moment. 'I'd prefer that pizza you once offered me, at your place.'

'You would? Fine!' He sounded delighted, and drawing to a halt outside her door, he said, 'I'll be in touch.'

His parting kiss was brief but sensual before he pushed open the car door to let her out. Even as she waved goodbye, he was gone.

Slowly she went up to her own flat, glad not to meet anyone on the way. She was a confused mixture of disappointment, despair and elation. *What* had he been about to say to her before that call came? What had it to do with James? And how might the night have ended had it not been for Damien's unfortunate accident? She would have to curb her impatience and wait. But the build-up and the let-down was all too much. It broke her up, and the tears would not be kept back.

Before going on duty at one o'clock the following day Fiona had lunch with Lois in the hospital canteen. And Lois was feeling particularly cheerful because Martin had telephoned her that morning.

'I was quite prepared for things to cool between us now that he's left here,' she said, 'but they haven't. His family are throwing a party for his sister's twenty-first, at Henley. And he's asked me to go. Can't be bad!' she beamed, seasoning her vegetable soup and stirring. 'How did you get on with Rory last night?'

'I didn't.' Fiona broke open her roll and buttered it. 'Sadly it came to a hasty conclusion soon after we left Molly. Did you hear that Damien Crewe had an accident?'

'No! Serious?'

Fiona shrugged. 'I don't know much about it yet, but serious enough for them to send for Rory just as we got back to his flat. A dislocated shoulder and a fractured elbow, he said. So I imagine you may find Damien in Paget when you get back there.'

'Oh, dear!' Lois put on a sympathetic face. 'That'll keep him out of action for a bit. Spoiled your evening too. You really like Rory, don't you?'

'In a word, yes. But it's probably a waste of good

emotion. In an oblique sort of way he told me I was too young for him.' Fiona took a bite of cheese and tomato. 'Oh! I'm fed up with thinking about him. I'm going to concentrate on my new job and make a really good go of it.'

'You do that. There's more to life than men,' her friend declared.

Fiona smiled wanly. 'But they do add a bit of spice to the proceedings. Anyway, wasn't it a stroke of luck, this sister's job coming up? At least it's something I can get my teeth into. I've been thinking of what improvements I can set in motion,' she mused. 'Like restarting the training programme for new staff nurses. None of them knows how to stitch or plaster, which is inclined to hold things up. Molly was a love, but she had let things slide.' Fiona's eyes twinkled. 'Bet you didn't know she plays the clarinet—and she's got a boyfriend?'

On the staff notice-board, which they passed going back to their respective work places, there was typed confirmation of Fiona's new appointment, and that at last made it seem real.

'I can't help being rather glad that Aileen will be leaving before long,' Fiona admitted. 'She's the one person I'd have been likely to have trouble with.'

It had been a quiet morning, Bea told Fiona when she arrived to take over. Usually Saturdays were busy, but they could still expect sports injuries later in the day.

Adrian sauntered into the office to talk to Fiona, Damien's accident still the subject of interest.

'He slipped on a patch of ice going home last night. Landed on his elbow, fractured the olecranon process, and put his shoulder out. Rory had him in Theatre and pinned the fragment.'

'Poor Damien,' she sympathised. 'It must have been very painful. I'll pop up to see him at teatime.'

The afternoon continued quiet. There were the usual sprained ankles, and minor cuts for stitching, and an elderly gentleman with severe abdominal pains who was admitted for observation.

During her tea break Fiona went up to Paget Ward and asked Anna's permission to see Damien.

'Yes, go ahead,' the sister said. 'He's in the side-ward, feeling rather sorry for himself. He'll be pleased to see you.'

Fiona knocked on his door and put her head in. Well supported with pillows, the casualty officer had been lying with his eyes closed. His shoulder was strapped and his injured elbow supported at right angles in a sling.

He opened his eyes as she asked, 'All right for me to come in?'

'Fiona, how nice of you to come,' he murmured weakly.

She crossed to the bedside and pulled out a stool. 'Poor you, what a rotten thing to happen. How are you feeling?'

'Lousy. God! It was excruciating, Fiona. You've no idea—I shall have much more sympathy with patients after this.'

She smiled. 'Yes, it's different being on the receiving end.'

He picked up her hand which was resting on the counterpane. 'This is all your fault, you know?'

'My fault—why?'

'Well, if you'd come back to my place as I suggested, I'd have been holding your hand or your arm, and I shouldn't have gone down.'

'You'd probably have had me down as well,' Fiona laughed, 'then we'd both have broken bones.'

'As it is, you decided to break my heart instead,' he returned dolefully.

'What a load of rubbish. Anyway, here you are with nice little nurses to come and check your pulse and make a fuss of you. How long will you be here, has Rory said?'

'Could be a week to ten days. Until he's sure everything's hunky-dory. No ischaemic problems and my hand in working order. Can't afford to have my hand impaired if I'm going to be a surgeon.' Damien wriggled his fingers slightly. 'You don't think they look blue, do you?'

Fiona smiled. 'No. Your trouble is you know too much. I'm sure Rory did a good job.'

'Yeah. He's got a nice way with him—gives one confidence.'

'So look on the bright side,' she encouraged. 'Now you'll have some free time to brush up on your studies for the fellowship. Well, I must get back to A and E and hope they haven't filled up all the cubicles in my absence.'

He squeezed her hand. 'Come and see me again?'

'OK, although I don't suppose you'll be lacking visitors.' With a farewell wave she left, only to find herself confronted outside by the consultant.

'What's this?' He studied her with a cryptic smile. 'Visiting the sick are we?'

'Well, I had to show some concern for the poor guy, didn't I?' she returned, her pulse beginning its usual clamour. 'We do work together. He's worrying about his hand. Were you able to do a good job?'

'Yes, I think so. We'll be watching his progress.' Rory paused, his eyes holding hers. 'Effie, with Imran away I shall be pushed for time this week, but I should be very glad if we could make a definite date for next Saturday.'

'Fine. I'll look forward to it,' she said.

'And is it still to be a pizza, at my place?'

She nodded. 'Suits me.'

'All right. I shall come and pick you up. Then you won't be able to run away, should we disagree.'

Fiona smiled. 'Are you anticipating we might?'

'Anything's likely with you. Shall we say seven o'clock?' He squeezed her arm and disappeared into Damien's room.

The days that followed were also busy ones for Fiona, but the hours stretching ahead to her date with Rory seemed agonisingly slow. On her days off she did her shopping, buying some peach kid court shoes to go with her wedding outfit, and the standard black lace-ups and black tights to complement her sister's uniform. And she also bought a pot of bulbs to brighten the relatives' room.

Back on duty, she tackled the endless administrative jobs to be done as well as trying to maintain the smooth running of the department. Having to feel her way, Fiona went in early and stayed late. Somehow Christmas decorations got put up in the waiting area and maintenance men were called to fix the fuse in Resus and demanding doctors were placated and anxious relatives handled with compassion.

The Christmas Fayre on Saturday was another extra that had to be fitted in. Over a coffee break the staff discussed it, wondering whether there would be enough items to make a good show on their cake stall.

'Molly told me that Mary, on Reception, belongs to

the WI and she was going to ask some of her friends to
contribute. I'll ask her what we can expect,' Fiona said.

Going over to the motherly clerk on the reception
desk, she had barely started to talk when a young couple
walked up to her, plus a small boy carrying a parcel.

'Hello, Sister,' the father beamed.

'Hello!' Recognition lit Fiona's eyes. She stooped to
the six-year-old's level. 'It's Mark, isn't it? How's your
finger?'

'Better, thank you,' the child said. He handed her the
parcel. 'It's a present—it's chocolates.'

'Oh, you are kind. Thank you very much. I'll share
them with my friends.' She smiled. 'Did you catch your
aeroplane and have a good holiday?'

'Yes, it was grand,' his mother put in. 'We were sorry
we had to rush away that afternoon. We wondered if
there was anything we could do to show our
appreciation?'

'Oh, that's all right. It's what we're here for—emergencies. Er.. .' Fiona hesitated. 'You *could* come along
and support our Christmas Fayre on Saturday. Or
perhaps you could make us a cake? A and E have the
cake stall.'

The parents looked at one another and laughed. 'We
can do better than that,' the father said. 'I'm a baker.
I'll send you a batch of stuff. How's that?'

Fiona's mouth gaped. 'I don't believe it! Will you
really? That's terrific.' She turned to the receptionist.
'Did you hear that, Mary? We shall have the best stall
in the show.'

Fiona was on duty that weekend and was not able to get
over to the social centre until the Fayre was about to
close. The lucky ticket for Molly's Christmas cake had

just been drawn and the prize handed over to the gleeful winner.

'That raised a bomb,' enthused Bea, who had been responsible for selling the raffle tickets.

'And your friend the baker did us proud,' the receptionist joined in. 'We've done well.'

'Thanks, girls,' Fiona said. 'It'll buy a few of the things we can do with that the budget doesn't run to.'

Most of the stalls were now packing up, and after wandering round and chatting with some of the other helpers Fiona bought some padded coat-hangers and a decorative Christmas candle, and returned home to get ready for her date with Rory.

At eight o'clock that evening Fiona was still trying to convince herself that the occasion was for real. Here she was at last, alone with Rory, and no one to disturb them.

Evocative background music came from the CD player and Rory was smiling at her across the table, over the flickering Christmas candle which she had brought with her. 'I'm glad you chose to come here,' he said. 'I'm not on call, but in a restaurant we *might* have got caught up in someone else's drama—like last time.'

Their pizzas had been eaten, washed down with a glass of Chablis, without which Fiona doubted she could have managed, so tense was she in the highly charged atmosphere. 'Well, I thought you might prefer to relax at home for a change,' she said.

'Must have been telepathy,' he declared. 'I bought some custard tarts for afters—or there's ice-cream, or yoghurt if you like?'

She shook her head. 'I'm full. Perhaps later.'

'OK—I'll get coffee.' He carried their plates through to the kitchen.

She followed him with the wine glasses. 'This seems like where we left it last time,' she said merrily.

'Yes.' He gave a twisted smile and began to fill the kettle.

'You were going to tell me why you needed to talk to James about *me*. So?' Fiona prompted, a flurry of wings in her throat.

'Oh, that.' Rory put mugs on a tray. 'Well, it was all fine by him, I'm glad to say.'

She gave an exasperated sigh. 'Rory! You are *the* most infuriating person. What was fine by him?'

He took the milk from the fridge. 'I am.'

'O-oh!' she despaired. 'We *know* your good mates, but what has that got to do with me, for goodness' sake?'

'Quite a lot.' At last he stopped fiddling around and came to put his hands on her shoulders, his compelling eyes seeking hers. 'Effie, you know I live my life by my own standards—I don't need other people's approval, but I should be sorry to cause family friction. I'm delighted to say there wasn't any.'

Fiona frowned, her bones melting at his touch. 'Why should there be?'

'Because, my darling. I'm so much older than you. And because, when we stand at the altar with your brother and his bride, I shall be wishing it were you and me.' He caught her in a close embrace. 'The truth is, I love you so much, it hurts,' he said hungrily. 'I believe I've been getting the right signals from you. *Please* tell me I'm not wrong.'

He had said it! He had actually said that he loved her. It was so amazingly unbelievable she didn't know whether to laugh or cry. She found she was doing a little of both. 'Oh, Rory! I've loved you for ages—you know I do,' she choked, wreathing her arms about his neck, her heart full to bursting.

'Sweetheart, don't cry!' He kissed the tears that overflowed. 'I want to love and cherish you for the rest of our days.' And he took her mouth with infinite tenderness, and then with a depth of passion which left no doubt of his burning desire.

They forgot about coffee and presently they lay in each other's arms on the sofa, exchanging confidences amid the sweet caresses of newly found love.

'I was mad about you even when I was thirteen,' Fiona told him, her eyes misty with longing. 'Meeting you again after all these years simply brought it back to life. The problem was, I did wonder if you were still not over Corinne. I've been going through hell, waiting for you to make up your mind.'

'My dearest, darling, adorable girl,' he murmured, stroking her hair, 'Corinne is my past. I'll always think of her with love. But one can't live with ghosts. I want you to be my present and my future for as long as I breathe.'

They kissed again with growing rapture.

'Eleven years is more than a decade,' he said, after a while. 'Tell me I'm not out of line—stealing your youth?'

'Don't be silly. Of course not. I prefer men to boys. When did you—what made up your mind to ask me— in the end?'

'When I saw that crushed white car on the motor- way—and prayed that you weren't in it. Melodramatic though that may sound, it was then I knew that I couldn't live without you. Damien Crewe making a play for you finally convinced me.'

'Thank you, Damien,' she murmured.

'Marry me?' he asked.

She glowed with happiness. 'Oh, what lovely words. Say it again?'

Rory slid off the sofa and went down on to one knee. 'Marry me!'

'Yes, please. When?'

He pulled her down on to the rug beside him. 'If only I could whisk you off to Gretna Green this minute. But they don't do things with such haste any more. In any case, I suppose we ought to observe the conventions. Your mother would never forgive me if I cheated her out of her only daughter's wedding.' He rained kisses over her face, her neck, her throat. 'Shall we make it in the spring, to give her time to get over her son's?'

Fiona eased herself against the seductive warmth of his long body. 'I'll try to wait that long, but I'm finding you terribly addictive.'

'I aim to get you so hooked on me you'll never want to look at another guy,' he growled.

Their mouths united in mutual ecstasy.

Yesterday was gone. Today was new and full of promise as they lingered, making plans, exchanging the sweet absurdities of love.

# — MEDICAL ♥ ROMANCE —

The books for enjoyment this month are:

**THE DOCTOR'S VISITOR** Alice Grey
**MAJOR INCIDENT** Grace Read
**ROGUE VET** Carol Wood
**MORE THAN MEMORIES** Judith Worthy

♥ ♥ ♥ ♥ ♥

## Treats In store!

Watch next month for the following absorbing stories:

**LOVE BLOOMS** Christine Adams
**HIGHLAND FLING** Margaret Barker
**A CASE OF MAKE-BELIEVE** Laura MacDonald
**THE RELUCTANT HEART** Elisabeth Scott

# Discover the thrill of 4 exciting Medical Romances - FREE

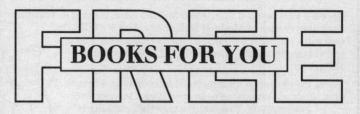

**FREE**

## BOOKS FOR YOU

In the exciting world of modern medicine, the emotions of true love acquire an added poignancy. Now you can experience these gripping stories of passion and pain, heartbreak and happiness - with Mills & Boon absolutely FREE! AND look forward to a regular supply of Medical Romances delivered direct to your door.

❧ ❧ ❧

Turn the page for details of how to claim 4 FREE books AND 2 FREE gifts!

# An irresistible offer from Mills & Boon

Here's a very special offer from Mills & Boon for you to become a regular reader of Medical Romances. And we'd like to welcome you with 4 books, a cuddly teddy bear and a special mystery gift - absolutely FREE and without obligation!

Then, every month look forward to receiving 4 brand new Medical Romances delivered direct to your door for only £1.70 each. Postage and packing is FREE! Plus a FREE Newsletter featuring authors, competitions, special offers and lots more...

This invitation comes with no strings attached. You may cancel or suspend your subscription at any time and still keep your FREE books and gifts.

It's so easy. Send no money now but simply complete the coupon below and return it today to:

**Mills & Boon Reader Service, FREEPOST, PO Box 236, Croydon, Surrey CR9 9EL.**

- - - - - - - - - - **NO STAMP NEEDED** - - - - ✂ - -

**YES!** Please rush me 4 FREE Medical Romances and 2 FREE gifts! Please also reserve me a Reader Service subscription. If I decide to subscribe, I can look forward to receiving 4 brand new Medical Romances every month for only £6.80 - postage and packing FREE. If I choose not to subscribe, I shall write to you within 10 days and still keep the FREE books and gifts. I may cancel or suspend my subscription at any time simply be writing to you.

I am over 18 years of age.          Please write in BLOCK CAPITALS

Ms/Mrs/Miss/Mr _____  EP54D

Address _____

_____

_____ Postcode _____

Signature _____

mps
MAILING
PREFERENCE
SERVICE